ELLIOTT

WOLF SONG
THE JOURNEYS CONTINUE

ISBN-10: 1499735235
ISBN 13: 9781499735239

Chapter 1

NEW HOME 2126

It had now been twenty years since the day the old world died and a new one was born..

There were now approximately twenty three thousand people listed as residents in New Home. Another twelve thousand resided in New Home South as the settlement in the former state of Alabama has chosen to call itself.

A central government had been established at a convention which had been held in Ames. The convention had not written a constitution but had decided to wait until the total population reached fifty thousand. The convention had written some rules which were to be incorporated into the constitution when it was written. The old state boundaries were to be ignored. There were no more states. They would retain the names and boundaries of the existing counties. There would be no more states and the areas would be identified as Provinces with a governor and small legislature for each. Not willing to totally break with the past, the new entity was to be called The United Provinces of America. When any area attained a population of twenty thousand it could establish Provincial boundaries and request recognition from the central government.

Since Boone was centrally located in New Home it was chosen as the seat of government for both New Home and the United Provinces. To insure that a citizen run government was maintained no person could serve more than two terms in any office or combination of offices. In addition no person could run for office more than three times. There would be no professional politicians. All judges would be nominated by the President for a term of six years and could not serve more than two terms. All other offices were to be three year terms. The convention had made no provision for a prison system. They simply did not have the resources or manpower to operate a system. The rules were those laid out by Jack Wilson. There were only three options. Shunning, banning or the death penalty could be ordered and only by a unanimous vote of a three member panel of judges.

Chapter 2 ----- 2126

MOBILE

Chris was excited. This would be his first flight to the Deep South. His flying had been sharply curtailed in the past few years. He had been elected to the convention in Ames and three growing children had his interest and kept him busy. The little ship he had seen in Bellingham had been in contact with the New Home South people and was scheduled to arrive in Mobile in two days. For ten years there had been no contact with the ship which had been named Discovery. It had long been assumed the ship been lost somewhere in the vast Pacific. Ten days ago a radio signal had been picked up and contact with the Discovery established. She had been off the coast of Florida, headed north in the hope of finding survivors along the east coast. She had reversed her course and was now in the Gulf of Mexico headed for Mobile. Chris was to fly to Mobile to pick up the skipper, four or five of the crew plus any who were in need of medical attention. Everyone was amazed to hear of the ship's survival and was anxious to learn the story of the ten year voyage.

Chris had hoped Pete would make this flight with him. Pete's eyesight had begun to deteriorate over the past two years and corrective lenses didn't do much to improve his distance vision. He had stopped flying solo and seldom flew even as a co-pilot. He was philosophical about it saying he had spent over thirty years at the controls and it was time to let the youngsters take over. Carol and the children went with Chris to the airport with Chris Jr. asking several times why he couldn't go on the trip. He loved flying with his dad and had trouble waiting until he was sixteen. His parents had told him he had to be that age before he could start flying lessons. Chris was in the air by 8:00 am. He set a southeast course to intersect the Mississippi at Hannibal, MO. He would then follow the river south to Vicksburg before turning southeast again for Mobile. The flight was about five hours so Chris was on the ground by mid-afternoon and was assured the plane would be fueled and ready to go by eight the next morning.

He was driven to what had been a Coast Guard base where the ship was scheduled to tie up the next morning. He was assigned a room, shown where the dining hall was located and given directions to where the Discovery would tie up. Everything was located within a short walk so he had no need for a vehicle. He sat in his room reading until supper time. The dining room was small, having only five tables. He asked two men and a woman if he could join them and was invited to take the vacant chair. As they introduced themselves it turned out one of the men was Jack Myers the Governor of New Home South. The woman was his daughter and the other man, named Will Benson was his secretary. Chris who had developed an almost photographic memory of the genealogy charts had a sudden flash of insight. He told Jack they were distant cousins. He said, "if you go back six generations you grandmother and my grandfather from that generation were sister and brother." When there was a lull in the conversation Will Benson who appeared to be in his early twenties uttered the statement, "you're the walking dude, aren't you?" Chris didn't understand the statement and asked what he meant. Will told him a group of people were compiling a history of the days since 2106. He added that there was an entire chapter devoted to the man who had walked the west. Chris admitted he had taken some memorable hikes but he by no means had covered the west. He told them if they wanted a really epic story of walking they should listen to the disc of his wife's walk out of the

Yucatan all the way to Bellingham. Jack told Chris he was planning a trip to New Home in the next month on Province business and if Chris could find time they could discuss family.

The next day at 10:00 am horns and whistles began to sound and Chris walked to the pier to see the Discovery being nudged into the dock by a small tug which had been put in working order. The men lining the ship's rail were as disreputable looking as the ship itself. Every man of them had long hair and a beard. Their clothing was patched and stained and they were weeping. Once the ship was secured to the pier a portable gang plank was rolled up and attached to the rail. It took a half hour to get the ship shut down and the reactors put in stand-by mode. The skipper finally appeared at the rail and invited whoever was in charge to come aboard. Jack Myers and the woman who was in charge of the Mobile contingent, Lori Shapiro, walked up the ramp and introduced themselves. The skipper, Mike Dunbar, simply said, "We are pleased to be home, we have detailed logs to explain our voyage and we would very much like to hear what has occurred during our absence." Jack explained there would be no de-briefing until the skipper and part of his crew were flown to New Home to meet with a committee to hear their story. A crew would be put aboard the ship to act as caretakers with strict orders that nothing of a personal nature was to be touched. The present crew would be provided comfortable quarters, new clothing and doctors to deal with any medical issues. In addition they would be provided transportation to any of the settled areas where they might choose to live. Jack then added that if the ship was still seaworthy there might be more missions to be undertaken and the present crew would be given first choice for those assignments. Mike told Jack the first thing the men wanted was access to a shower followed by new clothing and a barber. The water plant on the Discovery had gradually lost its ability to produce fresh water. There was enough for drinking, cooking and little else. The men had stopped shaving and bathing had been reduced to a spit bath every couple of weeks. Mike's words were, "We are dirty and smell bad." Out of the original crew of forty-two, seven had died or lost their lives in various ways. The ship's log books were placed in a case for Mike and each of the crew gathered what personal belongings they wanted to take.

The crew then boarded a bus and was driven to the U. of South Alabama where rooms were waiting for them. Four barbers were on hand and over the next five hours every one of the crew was shaved and had his hair trimmed. Each of them opted for a short military style buzz cut and when the barbers had finished one of the seamen commented that there was enough hair to stuff a mattress. They were then directed to the clothing center where each was issued two complete sets of clothing plus underwear, socks and shoes. Two hours later when they emerged from their rooms for supper they were a very different looking group than when they had filed off the ship in late morning. The dining room was set up cafeteria style and the men were thrilled at the variety of fresh fruit and vegetables being served. Jack addressed the group while they ate and told them they would have a day to try and regain their land legs before they had to start considering their futures. He asked Mike to select four of the crew to accompany him on the flight for the subsequent debriefing in New Home. The rest of the crew would be free to spend their time as they chose. When Mike returned from New Home the opinion of the crew would be vital in determining the future of the Discovery. Two days later the "Ugly Bird" lifted off at sunrise for the flight north. Mike had chosen the First Mate, Navigator, Chief Engineer and Doctor who had also served as the Chief Cook for much of the voyage. All of the seamen were from the west coast and none of them had ever seen the Mississippi. When the plane approached the river at Vicksburg Chris could hear the conversations from the passenger compartment change to a series of oohs and aahs. He thought this reaction was rather strange for a group which had just spent the better part of ten years on the Pacific Ocean. The flight was uneventful and they touched down at the Perry strip before noon. Chris got in his little truck for the drive home and the seamen were taken to the lunch room for a sandwich before going on to Boone.

Chapter 3 ----- 2126

When Chris arrived home the place was in an uproar. The horses were running in circles in the pasture. The cattle were all standing together staring into the timber and not twenty yards from the driveway lay a dead calf. When Chris drove up to the yard gate there was Carol sitting on the deck with the Marlin across her lap. Chris pointed to the rifle and Carol replied with one word, "cougar." Carol went on to tell Chris the three children had taken Dog for a walk out to the end of the driveway. They had turned the corner to see the cat with its teeth buried in the throat of the calf and the calf still thrashing about. Dog had begun barking and started to go after the cat. He changed his mind and returned to take up a protective position in front of the kids. The cat had released the calf then snarled and loped off into the timber. The children had rushed back to the house with their story. Carol took the Marlin out of the gun safe and loaded it. She had then given the kids firm instructions to stay in the house with Dog even if they heard gunshots. She had then walked out to the pasture. The calf was dead, apparently from a broken neck and Carol had returned to the house to take up her post on the deck. Chris changed his clothes, took the rifle and walked out to where the calf lay. He then walked the edge of the timber for a quarter of a mile on each side of the house without seeing anything of the cat. Carol had called all three neighbors because all of them had children the age of her own and pets as well. There would be no unsupervised outside play until the cat was eliminated. When Chris returned to the house he called Jack Wilson.

There was an older man who lived in the timber outside Redfield. He was something of a recluse and seldom appeared in town unless he was out of some basic commodity such as salt or flour. He had a pack of hounds and had gained a reputation for getting rid of problem cats and bears. He had been heard to say he preferred the company of his dogs to that of most people he knew. Jack told Chris the man's last name was Wilhelm and that he wasn't sure of the first name. Jack said he would get a message to the man and ask him to contact Chris. Two days later as Chris was walking out the door for a meeting with Brendon a ratty look-ing old truck pulled up to the gate. A gray haired man in patched jeans and shirt with beaded leather vest and moccasins got out. He didn't bother to introduce himself but opened the conversa-tion with, "I hear you have a cat problem." Chris told him he was correct and asked him his name. The old man said his name was Hans Wilhelm but just to call him Froache. He added that his grandfather had given him that name when he announced that he was going to study law in college. He said his Gramps was a German immigrant who hated lawyers. Froache was Gramps' word for worthless. He never called Hans anything else and the rest of the family had picked it up. Froache told Chris it was too far to drive every day and if Chris didn't mind he would set up camp a half mile east of the house. He said from the distance the barking of the dogs shouldn't be a problem. The only thing he would need from Chris was water every two or three days for himself and the dogs. Froache then told Chris he would need to take a couple of deer and perhaps a wild pig if there were any in the area. Chris assured him there was a plentiful supply of both deer and pigs and he could take all he wanted. Chris then asked Froache what he wanted in exchange for the hunting. The old man told him he didn't charge for hunting, only the results. He then asked if one of the hams from the Weddle smokehouse for each adult animal he took sounded fair. Froache also stipulated that he was to get the hides from the animals he killed. Chris walked down to the shop to show Froache where he could fill his water tanks and told him if he thought of anything else not to hesitate to ask. Froache told Chris if there was a cougar or bear within five miles of his home his dogs would find it and it would cease to be a problem.

Chris and Brendon were scheduled to fly the STOL to Winterset to look into two separate situations. The first concerned the old covered bridges in the area. They were landmarks which had been in place for two hundred years. After many years of neglect they were all in danger of falling in. A decision needed to be made whether the manpower and materials could be spared for the restoration. None of them any longer carried traffic except for pedestrians and the occasional horse drawn farm wagon. All of the bridges would have to be dismantled so new pilings and support beams could be installed. It would be a labor intensive project and there had been much debate on the subject. After they had examined the bridges the ever practical Brendon voiced his opinion. He pointed out that if the roofs, pilings, support beams and decks were replaced with the composite material the bridges would be almost maintenance free for two hundred years minimum. He even offered to write the proposal for the panel which would make the decision on whether or not to proceed with the project.

The other matter which needed their attention was three long abandoned farms along the river. There were three families which wanted to move from Dallas County, clear the river bottom and farm it. The farms were adjacent to each other and had been subject to severe erosion in the past. There was a contingent of local people who favored leaving the land vacant and allowing it to return to a natural state. After looking at the properties Chris and Brendon were in agreement. There was a surplus of good farm land available and this particular tract should be left to revert to its original form. The three Dallas County families would not be happy with the decision but with the majority of New Home still open to anyone who wanted to claim and work the land it would impose no hardship on them.

When Chris returned home he found an urgent message from Jack Wilson. There was to be an emergency meeting of the Provincial Council at nine the next morning and it was imperative that Chris attend. The next day had been chosen for the monthly

Wolf Song supper which had been a tradition for the past ten years. If the adults seemed to take the day for granted Mavis never did. Nor did she allow the adults to treat it as just another day. It was always special and always fun. The four families had built a shelter house between the Hintz and Brown homes. It was open on the south side with a huge river rock fireplace, picnic tables and benches. They had installed one of the new wind turbines so there was power for lights and an electric grill. This was where the supper was held when the weather permitted. Chris asked Carol if she would call the other families and postpone the event for one day as he didn't know what time he would be finished with the meeting in Boone.

Jack called the meeting to order promptly at nine. He told the gathering there were three items on the agenda. First he had been informed that an attempt would be made to place a communication satellite in a stationary orbit over the equator. If successful it would make it possible to transmit radio, television and telephone signals over all of the North American continent. It would have the capacity to serve a population of more than twenty times the current number of people now known to exist. There was a standing ovation for this announcement and Jack added, "We're coming back folks, we're coming back." The second item concerned an apparent significant increase in seismic activity in the far west. At the present time there was no available instrumentation to adequately monitor the situation. There was a proposal to add additional fuel tanks to the "Ugly Bird" which would enable the plane to fly to California then turn north and follow the coast all the way to the Canadian border. From there it would turn for home. He wanted Chris to fly the mission but if Chris didn't wish to undertake the risky flight they would like to borrow his plane. Jack advised Chris to go home and discuss the flight with Carol before making up his mind. The third item on the agenda was a trial scheduled to start after this meeting was over. It was the first case in New Home involving the possible death sentence. It was concerned with two men caught in the act of attempting to rape a fifteen year old girl. The trial would be held here in the same room and Jack wanted everyone present to remain for the trial.

The room quickly filled to capacity and the three citizen judges took seats at the table in front of the room. Of the three judges two were women of middle age and the man was elderly and walked with a cane. One of the women appeared to be the spokesperson for the trio. She was seated in the middle and it was she who said, "Bring in the accused." Two men were led in. Their hands were tied behind their backs and their ankles shackled so they were forced to shuffle when they walked. One of them was a big man of perhaps fifty years. Both of his eyes were swollen and black. His nose was bent to one side as if broken. The other was a young slightly built man whose right arm was in a splint. His eyes were red as if from crying. The judge then asked the witnesses to come forward. Two very nervous young men stepped to the front of the room. They were both obviously Indian and appeared to be no more than fifteen or sixteen years old. They were asked to explain what they had witnessed. The smaller of the two spoke first. He said the girl who had been attacked was his twin sister. She worked in the lunch room and had been asked to take a sandwich to the two workmen at the end of her shift. He and his friend had walked with her to the building where the men were working and waited outside while she took the food inside. They waited for what seemed a long time then went in to look for his sister. They heard noises from a back room and went to see what they were. They entered the room to see his sister, who had been stripped naked, with her ankles tied to the legs of a saw horse. The younger man was behind her grasping her wrists and had her bent over the saw horse. The big man was in front of her with his penis in his hand trying to enter her while shouting, "Hold her still." The boy picked up a piece of construction lumber and swinging as hard as he could hit the big man across the kidneys. When the man fell to the ground the boy kicked him in the face. The boy's friend had picked up a similar piece of wood and struck the smaller man across the arm breaking the arm. While both men were incapacitated the boys found some light rope and securely tied their hands and feet. The boys then helped the girl find her clothing, at least those articles which hadn't been ripped to shreds, and get dressed. The construction boss listened to their story and sent six men to bring the culprits to his office. They were held for two days in the Carroll city jail then driven to Boone for trial. The judge then asked the second boy if he had anything to add. He said no that it happened just as the first boy had related. The boys were excused and the judge asked the prisoners if they wished to speak. The older man spoke first. He said he knew what the judges were going to order and that he didn't understand what the flap was all about. It wasn't like the girl was a real person, she was an Indian and not really human. He didn't care to live in a place which gave valuable land to people who were less than human. The younger man didn't really address the court but was weeping and repeating over and over, "I'm sorry, I promise it won't ever happen again." The judges excused themselves and were gone no more than fifteen minutes. When they filed back in and took their seats the younger man resumed saying, "It won't happen again." The judge interrupted him to say, "No, it certainly will not. The verdict is guilty. The sentence is death to be carried out immediately." She continued by saying, "It is obvious that racial bigotry did not die with most of the world but we must do what we can to eliminate it." The men were led out to what looked like a child's sand box. They were made to kneel and then Cookie stepped forward from the edge of the crowd. He raised an automatic pistol and fired two quick shots. The judge then told four men to dispose of the bodies by leaving them in a secret location where the vultures and coyotes could dispose of them. She said they didn't deserve to be buried in the good earth which held the bodies of so many honorable men.

Chris was home in time to have supper with his family. After the children were in bed, he and Carol talked late into the night. The children were the first topic. All three were doing very well in school and in another year a decision would have to be made whether to transport them to Perry every school day or to enroll them in the boarding program which was now in place. Carol didn't know if she was ready to spend that much time away from the three whom she still referred to as her babies. They put that issue aside as they had a year to decide. They discussed the flight to the west which Jack had asked Chris to undertake. He wasn't excited about the prospect of such a long flight. It would have to start and end in darkness. He felt it was asking a lot from the plane he had been flying for over twenty years. Maintenance on the aircraft had been of the highest quality but it was still an old plane. On the other hand he was the most qualified pilot available to make the flight and he felt obligated to do all he could to help the community. Carol asked if it would be a solo flight and Chris told her that just wasn't possible. They then talked about possible co-pilots. Pete would have been the first choice and would go if asked but Chris didn't want to put added strain on Pete's failing eyesight. Chris thought of Brendon who had several hours at the controls of the plane although he had never made any takeoffs or landings. Brendon would no doubt be happy to make the flight but there was Phoebe to consider. If she made a strenuous objection Brendon would defer to her wishes and stay home as Chris would do if Carol objected. Chris made up his mind to bring up the subject at the Wolf Song supper the next evening.

Jack called Chris early the next morning and asked him to come to the airport. When Chris arrived Jack was waiting with three men who he introduced as aircraft designers and engineers. They had already spent two hours examining the "Ugly Bird" and thought it could be modified to carry out the mission Jack had in mind. They wanted to extend the nose three feet to make room for a camera and a thermal imaging device. They would add two fuel tanks on pylons under the wings plus a two hundred fifty gallon tank in the passenger cabin. They would need to remove some skin panels to see if the airframe was strong enough to support the additions they were contemplating. It would be a rush job and their crews would need to start immediately if they wanted to complete the work in the month Jack had allowed them. Chris cringed inwardly at the thought of what they were planning for his plane but gave his consent and left for home.

He spent most of the afternoon with his horses. All three of them were at least twenty-five years old. He tried to maintain a close watch on them for any sign of age related infirmities. So far they seemed to be in good health and he spent the early afternoon grooming and petting them.

When the families began gathering at the shelter Mavis was not with Brendon and Phoebe. Phoebe said Mavis had been in a dither all afternoon and told them she would be along later and that she had a surprise for them. Mavis was now nineteen and was a striking looking young woman. She had already studied and apprenticed with the Librarian in Perry and was in the process of opening a public library in Carroll. She was determined that every child of the Cheyenne people was going to read at a high level. As they were sitting down to eat a strange car drove up. Mavis jumped out of the passenger side and ran around to the driver's door. The young man who got out looked familiar to Chris but he couldn't put a name to the face. Mavis answered that question by asking the group if they remembered Jonathon. They all did except Jackie who had never met him. Mavis told them Jonathon had a question for her father and Uncle Chris. At this point Phoebe stood up grasped Jonathon in a hug and then addressed her daughter. "For goodness sakes Mavis, Jonathon doesn't need our approval to marry you. You made up your mind ten years ago and this young man never had a chance to do anything else." Mavis looked to her dad who nodded yes. She turned to Chris and told him she needed his permission as well. Chris didn't quite understand but he told her, "of course, if it's what you want. Mavis kissed her father then Chris and thanked them both. Phoebe told the young couple to fill their plates and sit down as she was hungry. Melinda, who had been quietly observing while all of this took place, stood up, raised her glass of apple cider and announced she wanted to make a toast. First, she said, to the young couple who were about to begin their life together and secondly to Chris. She told them she understood totally the love and respect Mavis felt for Chris. Turning to Chris she told him that kind of devotion was the result of his being a very, very good man. As they ate a lively conversation was carried on. The children were asked about school and what they were studying. Mel told of seeing Froache and his dogs moving across the pasture. She said he had waved to her but had not spoken. The trial and

14

executions of the previous day were reviewed. Carol commented that it was a harsh law but such people had no place in their community. There was much speculation about what new information which the debriefing of the seamen might bring to light. During a lull in the conversation Phoebe turned to Chris and in a casual manner asked him if he was going to take Brendon as his co-pilot on his flight to the west. Chris was stunned by the question. The flight was supposed to be a secret and Chris turned to Carol to ask if she had spoken to Phoebe. Before he could speak Carol told him he leak had not come from her. Phoebe laughed and told them nothing in the community was secret; that she had known about the flight within two hours after Jack had talked to Chris. Phoebe then told Chris he might as well take Brendon with him because if he didn't Brendon would just mope from now until a month after the flight was over. Chris announced that this was going to be his last long flight. When it was over he intended to limit his flying to regional hops in one of the small planes.

Two days later, on the first of May, Chris drove to the airport to check the progress of the work on his plane. The engineer in charge of the project, Lance Anderson, met him at the hangar door. He told Chris not to be shocked at the appearance of the plane. It would all go back together very nicely plus the computer and slide rule figures indicated it would have better flight characteristics and the elongated nose would actually improve the range by three percent. All of the nose skin panels had been removed as well as the outer one third of each wing. The mechanics were in the process of removing some of the nose frame in preparation for extending it. Rascal was present and it was apparent he was highly agitated. Those people were ruining his airplane. To distract him Chris asked if the twin jet Pete had always flown was prepared for flight. Rascal told him all they needed to do was wash the windows and top off the fuel tanks. Chris asked him to have it ready at eight the next morning. He wanted to get Brandon more multi-engine time even though it was not the same plane he would be flying.

They flew every day for the next week and Chris would have been comfortable to let Brendon fly solo. Chris talked with Pete who came to the airport and rode through several flights with Brendon. After the fifth landing Pete patted Brendon on the shoulder and told him to go make four take offs and landings while Pete watched from the tower. When Brendon finally taxied to the hangar he was met by Pete and Chris. Pete shook Brendon's hand and said, "Take good care of that plane, it now belongs to you."

The "Ugly Bird" was rapidly taking shape and Chris thought the stretched nose actually improved the appearance of the plane. Jib replaced the nose art and made it larger than the original had been. He even added a smaller version to the outside of each wing tank. All that was left to do was install the camera and thermal sensing device. Jack sent two men in the jet to check the runway at the old Air Force base at Rapid City in case it was needed for an emergency stop by Chris and Brendon on their long flight. The men came back without landing to report the runway appeared to be covered with several inches of dust which was probably of volcanic origin. They had also checked the fields at Pierre and Sioux Falls and reported them clear and usable.

Chapter 4 ----- 2126

On May 20th Lance pronounced the plane ready for a test flight. Chris and Brendon immediately began a series of test hops. With the added weight of the new fuel tanks the take-off and landing rolls were a little longer. The plane didn't seem quite as nimble in the air but Chris couldn't detect any significant changes. After four days of test hops it was time to check out the camera and thermal imager. From an altitude of fifteen thousand feet the camera was supposed to cover an area about two miles wide with the thermal device covering slightly less. They took off and flew east to the Mississippi which they followed north. They crossed Minnesota so they passed over Minneapolis and continued west to the Missouri River at Pierre. They then followed the Missouri all the way to Sioux City where they turned south east for home. Both the camera and the thermal device were digital so the image storage capacity was huge. They had been set to snap an image every two minutes so there would be hundreds to examine. The picture clarity was very detailed and the thermal images showed every river and lake where the water was colder than the surrounding soil. It was hoped the imager would pick up the heat signature of magma if it was near the surface. The day before they were scheduled to leave Chris tried to sleep most of the day. Take-off was planned for two a.m. with their return estimated at ten that night. At their planned cruising speed of two hundred seventy MPH it would allow them time and fuel to make extra passes over areas they thought required more scrutiny. Chris and Brendon drove to the airport together. Arriving at midnight they found Rascal and Jib just finishing cleaning the windshield. They announced the plane as ready as they could make it. There was ample coffee in a large thermos jug plus juice and sandwiches for three meals. Jack and Martha were present to wish them a safe trip and Jack warned them against flying through any ash clouds they might encounter. They had agreed to fly in four hour shifts with Chris taking the first one.

They took off at precisely two a.m., climbed to fifteen thousand feet and both men put on oxygen masks. Chris dialed the autopilot to a heading for southern California. Brendon draped a towel across his eyes and tried to sleep. Chris had a cup of coffee in a thermal cup which he sipped on as he looked at the stars and the dark landscape below. At a little after four a.m. Chris saw lights on the ground. They were in a place where there should be no lights. It was still too dark to see details so Chris turned on the camera and the thermal device hoping one or both would divulge something not visible to his eyes. Just before five, Brendon sat up and looked around. He got out of his seat and went to make use of the toilet and splash some cold water on his face. He returned to his seat and announced he was ready for the day. He offered to take the controls but Chris told him he was good for another hour and would finish his shift. Brendon did the mental math and asked if it was Phoenix he could see off the right wing. By six Brendon had eaten his breakfast sandwich and a cup of applesauce. He poured a cup of coffee and Chris gave him control of the plane. After Chris visited the toilet he washed his face with cold water, took his breakfast out of the cooler and returned to his seat. When they crossed the Colorado River at Yuma Chris turned on the camera and thermal imager. He set the controls to take three recordings per minute. There would be some overlap of the pictures but he wanted to cover the entire area which they would be flying. They were just north of San Diego when they first saw the Pacific. Brendon was flying the plane manually and began his turn to the north. They both became aware that the coastline didn't look natural. Where there should have been beaches and towns there were rugged cliffs and roads which ended in thin air. Chris pulled the map case from under his seat and extracted the maps for California. It quickly became apparent that great chunks of the coast were gone. In some places strips as wide as fifteen miles had simply disappeared. The only place they could have gone was into the sea. Brendon put the plane on autopilot and helped Chris compare the landscape to what the map told them it should be. In some areas there were great rifts in the land. Sometimes close to the water and in other places ten to fifteen miles inland. As they continued north the devastation below continued as well. When they arrived over San Francisco the city wasn't there. The entire peninsula north of San Jose was gone. The Pacific now lapped against the shores of Oakland. They turned and made another pass over the area then continued north. They turned inland and followed I-5. As they passed over Mt. Shasta it appeared as if three to four thousand feet of the mountain was gone. A path of gray ash fanned out to the southeast of the mountain as far as they could see. As they crossed into Oregon they turned slightly east and more or less flew up the crest of the Cascades. As they passed over Crater Lake they were amazed again. There was no lake but a new mountain protruding at least a thousand feet above the crater rim. They continued north and as they passed Mt. Hood saw only a blackened stump of the once majestic mountain. This scenario continued all the way up across Washington. Mt. Adams was gone and from a distance it appeared as if Mt. St. Helens had erupted again. Mt. Rainier was a stump and they didn't wish to contemplate the damage downstream from that event. Finally, Mt. Baker in the far north was all but erased from any future maps. Both Baker dams had failed and the ensuing floods had wiped out all the little towns along the Skagit River. The men turned the plane east and crossed the Cascades. They flew over Grand Coulee Dam and observed many gaping cracks in the giant structure. There was water pouring from some of the fissures and it seemed obvious that sooner or later the dam would collapse. They set a compass bearing on the autopilot to take them over Yellowstone Park and let the plane fly itself. Two hours later, they crossed the Tetons and turned left to go north across the park. The first thing they noticed was the absence of steam from the many usual sources. What had been a big depression with rounded contours on the rim now seemed much deeper with sharp edges from freshly fallen cliff faces. It appeared that water was beginning to fill the basin as the rivers flowing out of the park had been dammed by falling rocks. It was two very sober and quiet men who put the plane on a course for New Home and settled back to let the auto pilot do the flying for the next few hours. They had plenty of fuel so they increased their speed to three hundred fifty MPH. They were ready to be home with their families.

When they approached Perry, Rascal had the runway and taxi lights turned on. It was a most welcome sight to both men. What was even more welcome was the sight of their wives and children when they shut down the engines and climbed out of the plane.

Chapter 5 ----- 2126

Jack was there to meet the plane and he told Chris and Brendon to rest the next day then be in Boone the following day to report on their flight. He told them there would be a short report on the voyage of the Discovery plus the weather people had a rather startling announcement about the growth of the ice up in the polar region.

When Chris arrived home he found Mavis, Jonathan, Jackie and Pete waiting for him. Pete said he would speak first as his message was short and he knew they had family matters to discuss. Pete began by saying they needed another pilot and that had had a promising candidate. He said he had been giving Jonathan lessons in one of the small planes and he was a very apt pupil. What he wanted was for Chris to continue the lessons in both the twin jet and the "Ugly Bird". The day would come when either Chris or Brendon would not be able or available for a flight and they needed to be prepared for that day. Chris agreed and said they would set up a schedule for training flights.

As soon as Pete and Jackie left for home, Mavis turned to Chris and announced that she and Jonathan were going to be married the following week. They were going to have the ceremony in a little country church south of Dawson. The church had been rebuilt ten years ago and had been holding weekly services since then. She wanted both her father and Chris to walk her down the aisle. She had already asked her father and he had given his complete approval. Chris asked if he was going to need to hunt up a suit and tie. Mavis laughed and said she would not recognize him with a tie, jeans and a shirt would do nicely. With that settled, Chris collapsed into bed and for the first time in years didn't hear a single note of wolf song that night.

The next morning Chris slept late. After he showered and dressed he walked out to the kitchen to find Carol putting his breakfast on the counter. As Chris sat down to eat Carol sat on the stool next to his and put her arm around his waist. She then said, "At the risk of spoiling your breakfast, how would you feel about having another baby in the house?" Chris was stunned and sat for a long moment before he asked her if she was sure. She nodded yes and he told her he was very pleased. Carol said, "It has only been a month but I swear I can feel her moving." They sat for a long time holding hands and not speaking. Chris finally kissed the top of Carol's head and told her thank you. He also told her that Grandpa John had always said that four children made the perfect sized family and that he would be pleased if he was here for the announcement.

Chapter 6 ----- 2126

Later that morning Chris had been out to stoke the smokehouse fire. As he was returning to the house a strange car pulled in the driveway. Chris waited for the driver to get out then walked over to greet him. The man looked vaguely familiar but Chris couldn't put a name to the face. His hair was gray and close cropped and his face was pale as if he hadn't been in the sun for months. As the man began to speak, it dawned on Chris that this was Froache, the bearded, longhaired old man who had been hunting the cougar. When Froache realized Chris hadn't known him he laughed and told Chris he almost didn't recognize himself after twenty years of long hair and a beard. He told Chris he had given up hunting and was going to return to the practice of law. He had given his dogs to a young neighbor who had been hunting with him for ten years and who was capable of taking over predator control in the area. He was going to move to the Carroll area and set up a law office. There was a lady who for years had been trading him finished leather goods for the hides of animals he had taken. She had forty acres of land along the Middle Raccoon River and had been trying to get him to move either into cabin of his own or in with her. Froache said he supposed he was going to need to marry her as it wouldn't seem proper for the first lawyer in town to be living with a woman out of wedlock. He told Chris the woman happened to be a Cheyenne and fifteen years younger. He said none of the tribe seemed to care that he was white and older and he sure hoped they didn't hold it against him for being an attorney. He then told Chris that he had eliminated two adult cougars and two half grown cubs. He had also taken two black bears and two cubs as well as five adult wolves from a pack between

Rippey and Grand Junction. Froache concluded that according to their agreement Chris owed him a bunch of hams but he would settle for one. He would consider the predators his gift to the community and the ham as a wedding gift from Chris. Chris took him to the smokehouse to pick out his ham and convinced him to take a slab of bacon and a rack of pork chops as well. As Froache was leaving he told Chris if he ever needed a lawyer his shingle would be hanging in Carroll and to look him up.

As the family was eating supper that evening Carol informed the children that they were to have a new baby sister in late January or early February. This announcement brought on a flurry of questions. How, why, what was her name going to be and who was going to name her? Carol laughed and told them they would learn the how in good time. The why was because she wanted another baby; and they would all work together to choose a name. Craig commented now the twins would have someone beside himself to boss around. Chris asked Craig if the twins really bossed him that much. Craig replied that they tried to. Chris told him he was too much like his Great-Grandpa John for anyone to boss him very much. The entire family spent the evening on the deck waiting to hear the nightly chorus from the wolves. When it was over they all retired.

Chris didn't sleep well. His mind was going over all that had happened since 2106 and how much remained to be accomplished if they were to create a viable, self-sustaining civilization.

Brendon arrived early next morning. Carol had invited him to have breakfast before he and Chris left for their trip to Boone. As they ate the two men discussed their flight to the west coast and what they had observed. When they arrived at the school where the meeting was to be held they were surprised at the number of people present. Jack explained that a number of them were scientists and technologists who had been reviewing the film and thermal images from their flight. Others were climatologists who had been studying the ice growth in the north. The four men from the Discovery were present plus two people form each county having a population greater than five hundred. The first item to be covered, were the images from the flight. The pictures were self-explanatory. The destruction in California was vivid and sobering. The stubs of the Cascade volcanoes were shown with pictures of their previous shapes beside them. The pictures of Grand Coulee Dam were also sobering and gasp provoking. The scientists who had reviewed the thermal images were next on the agenda. They explained that the southern part of California appeared to be sitting on a giant field of magma which was close to the surface and which was probably going to rise and that more of the area was going to slide into the Pacific. The seismographs were continuing to record massive earth movements and there was no way of predicting when they would end. One more major tremor would likely complete the destruction of Grand Coulee and no one knew the condition of the other Columbia River dams. If the other dams already had significant damage the collapse of Grand Coulee would most likely signal the end for all of them. The volcanic peaks in the Cascade Range were a puzzle. It appeared that the magma under the range had built up enough pressure that all of the volcanoes had blown up almost simultaneously after which the remaining magma had drained away. There was almost no heat signature under the range and no clue as to where the magma had gone. The Yellowstone Basin was another anomaly. The giant magma chamber under the area appeared to have drained away. The result of that event was that the floor of the basin had dropped about five hundred feet and the basin was going to become a giant lake. They wanted to recommend a second flight over the area in two months. This flight was to include all of the Columbia River dams plus the dams on the Snake River. They knew the flight was unlikely to occur but it could give them valuable insight on the future of the Northwest. Chris stood up and Jack asked if he wished to speak. Chris told them he and Brendon had seen no smoke, ash or steam issuing from any of the volcanoes or the Yellowstone area. What he really wanted to know was whether they had looked at the pictures he had taken at four o'clock on the morning of their flight. The photo expert stood up and apologized for omitting that information. He said the photos appeared to be of a rest stop on highway 287 in southeast Colorado which was lighted by a still functioning solar system. They had identified horses and wagons but no electrical or internal combustion vehicles. There were a few people visible and they appeared to be dark skinned. His best guess was that they were all or part of the Cheyenne tribe which had stayed on the Rio Grande when the rest moved to New Home. Jack then told the group that a second flight might not be needed. The group which had put up the communication satellite had a second rocket ready to go and was putting the finishing touches on a photo satellite which they would attempt to launch into a polar orbit. The satellite would have the capability of being steered and thus enable them to examine any area of the earth they wished to view.

The climatologists announced they would prefer to hold their report for three or four months until it was determined whether the new satellite launch was successful. Pictures from the satellite would help prove or disprove whether their forecast was accurate.

Jack took the floor again. He pointed out that it was late in the day and the report from the seamen was going to be lengthy. He suggested they stop for the day and meet again in a week. He and several others had urgent business in Mobile and would be gone for several days.

After the meeting adjourned, Jack asked Chris if he would fly another mission to the west if it was deemed necessary. Chris told him no. He had promised Carol he would make no more marathon flights and he meant to adhere to that promise. Jack then asked Chris if he would fly the group which was going to Mobile in two days. Again, Chris told him no but added that if Brendon wanted to fly the plane he would go along as co-pilot for a last check flight.

Chapter 7 ----- 2126

When Chris arrived at the airport in the morning he was surprised to see the twin jet out on the ramp with the "Ugly Bird" sitting in the hangar. Brandon was there with Jonathon but before Chris could speak to them Rascal hurried over. Rascal told Chris he had found cracks at the roots of both wings of the old plane and didn't think it should be flown until a thorough inspection could take place. Chris had learned to never question Rascal's judgment about the plane and readily agreed. Brendon suggested that Jonathon be the pilot for this flight with Chris in the other seat to judge his capability. Chris agreed and Brendon told him he was going to cut back on his flying hours in order to devote more time to his family and farm. He had already spoken with two of the men working his land and they had chosen two farms to move onto when they were finished working his land. Chris told him they would discuss it later and they set about preparing for the flight. Jack appeared with four men and introduced them as being from the weather group and two from the Board of Regents as the governing body had come to be called. Jack told Chris he wanted him to attend all of the meetings in Mobile. The flight was uneventful and Chris pronounced Jonathon ready to take over as Chief Pilot of the twin jet. They were met at the airport by Jack Myers and a contingent of a dozen people most of whom were carrying briefcases or thick folders of papers. Jack announced they would be meeting in rooms in a hotel adjacent to the airport. He told them to take two hours to eat and get settled into their rooms then they would be driven to the waterfront to see what was being done to the Discovery. Jack Wilson arranged for himself, Chris and Brendon to be assigned to a three bedroom suite with a kitchen and large sitting room. He told the two younger men they needed to talk that night before attending the meeting in the morning.

When they arrived at the waterfront they were greeted by the sight of the Discovery perched on blocks in a dry dock. She had been scraped and sand-blasted and was being prepared for painting. There were workers in and on the ship cleaning, painting and generally refurbishing the ship. The ship fitters had determined that the hull was as sound as when she was new. The nuclear engines still had ample fuel for another forty years. All the ship lacked to be seaworthy was two new propellers. A nearby shipyard was working on those by cutting down two props from larger ships. Jack Myers told him they had a proposed new mission for the ship which he would discuss in the meeting tomorrow.

That night for their supper they were treated to fish and prawns which were fresh off the boat that day. Both Brendon and Chris were so taken with the fresh seafood that they ate too much and then asked for more to take with them for a late snack. Jack reminded them the fish and prawns would be available the next day and perhaps they should wait until then. They reluctantly agreed and the three of them returned to their suite.

They settled into comfortable chairs and Jack opened the conversation. He told the two younger men they would be hearing some drastic suggestions at tomorrow's meeting but didn't elaborate. He told them he wanted to see their reaction to the proposals and suggestions without thinking about them overnight. Jack then brought up the subject of higher education. He told them it was past time to establish a college or university so the young people who wanted it could be educated in a chosen field. They were learning now but it was a hit and miss situation of one on one tutoring. They had world class scientists and philosophers in their population but they were getting older and several had already died. He said it was time to gather all that talent in one place and let the students come to them as a group rather than as individuals seeking tutoring. Jack then told them it would take a person with an uncommon amount of common sense to organize and put a school into operation and he said he had such a person in mind. He then turned to Brendon and told him if he would accept the responsibility, it was a task which would keep him busy for the rest of his working life. Brendon protested that he had very little formal education but Jack told him for this job they didn't need a man who could split atoms but one who could choose and direct people. Brendon said he would need to consult Phoebe to which Jack replied he had already talked with her and she was in complete agreement. Jack then told Brendon he would have to give up his farm but suspected that after tomorrow that would not be a consideration in any case. Brendon then asked if he could have some time to consider and Jack told him he had a week after they returned home. It would give Brendon time to talk with his wife and they could plan the future together.

Jack then turned his attention to Chris. He said he was seventy years old and he was tired. He wanted time to spoil the Wolf Song children as if they were his own grandchildren and he couldn't do it from his present position. He said that in less than two years they would be electing a President and it was his intention to nominate and campaign to place Chris in that position. He said Chris was known to and respected by everyone in New Home and electing him would be easy. In the meanwhile, he wanted Chris to become his Chief Aide for the next month then take over the job completely.

Two sobered men went to bed that night wondering what tomorrow was going to bring.

Jack Myers opened the meeting at nine the next morning. He started by telling them that every word would be recorded and a disc made available to anyone who wanted one. He then announced that he had just received a call from the Cape telling him the photo satellite had been launched at dawn and appeared to be functioning perfectly. The weather people were asked to speak next. Their first statement was that across the northern half of North America the average temperature had dropped four degrees in the past two years. They predicted the rate of temperature drop would increase and that within one hundred years the Midwest where most of the grain and food crops were grown would not sustain agriculture. It would simply be too cold. They explained that they had planned to make a prediction about the ice growth in the north but now wished to wait on photographs from the new satellite before addressing that subject. They did suggest that the people in authority begin considering moving the population center south sooner rather than later.

Jack Wilson took the floor to announce that he had copies of the report from the crew of the Discovery which he would leave with Jack Myers to distribute as he saw fit. He did say that pockets of people had been found in several locations and they should discuss possible efforts to contact them. He also announced his imminent retirement and that Chris was going to take over his post until a permanent government was established.

Jack Myers spoke again and told the group that a panel chosen by the Director of New Home South was recommending that the refitted Discovery be sent on a year's long voyage to visit the west coast of Africa, all of the Mediterranean Sea and the coast of Europe.

The meeting ended but the two Jacks plus Chris and an aide of Jack Myers talked late into the night. They agreed to name a ten member board to oversee the move of the population of New Home to the south. This board would have the authority to appoint people to direct the many aspects of the move starting with housing. Jack Wilson insisted they select a city as the new capital and that the organizing board be based there with the government to be formed around it. Chris suggested Montgomery as the new Capital. He commented there was a precedent for the choice, reminding the others it had been the first Capital of the Confederacy at the beginning of the Civil War. Jack Myers made the statement that the majority of people in the south seemed to favor the retention of both the names and boundaries of the old states as well as the name of the United States of America. This involved major decisions which would have to be made by means of a popular vote and both groups agreed to immediately distribute a ballot on the issue. The meeting ended with the decision made to meet again the next day to determine what topics needed to be on the ballot. As Jack and Chris were walking to their rooms, Jack remarked to Chris that he needed to start preparing himself to be the first President of the new United States. The next day Brendon was asked to attend the meeting. He was informed of the impending move of the New Home people to the south. He was then asked to serve as Chairman of the board which was going to oversee the move. He was told the establishment of a University would be put on hold until the move was complete or at least nearly so. Brendon suggested he be allowed to select a location and a president for the school. That man could start selecting staff for the school while the move was still in progress. That idea was approved and then they worked out the details and wording of what was to go on the ballots which would go out within the month.

On the flight home the next day the subject arose on what was to be done with the New Home people who refused to move south. They had only been settled for ten years and it was thought many of them would not wish to be uprooted again. The general opinion was that in two or three years the isolation and loneliness would force most of the stay behinds to change their minds and follow their former neighbors south.

On arriving home Chris and Brendon called a meeting of their Wolf Song neighbors and explained the dramatic changes which were looming. It was discussed that they would attempt to maintain their little community wherever they might settle, probably in the Montgomery area. They might all have to build new homes if they were going to remain together but all agreed it would be worth the cost.

Two days later, Mavis and Jonathon were married in the little country church. Gray Eagle and several other tribal members came for the ceremony.

Jack and Chris took the opportunity to explain to the Cheyenne about the upcoming changes. Gray Eagle was disappointed. He told them for the first time his people were at peace with the world and lived on land which nurtured them and which they loved. He told them if it was necessary his people would give up their new land and go where they could survive into the future. He did request they be allowed to settle together so they could maintain their tribal identity. Brendon, who was to oversee the move, assured him his request would receive a very high priority. Gray Eagle announced that he was stepping down as Chief but would wait until the move south was completed before turning over the leadership to a younger person.

During the wedding dinner Mavis asked her father and Chris if she and Jonathon would be allowed to move into the Wolf Song community. She was told of the impending move south and it was suggested the newly married couple wait until after the move to build or restore a house. They were informed that they would be welcomed into the little community wherever it might be.

Jack announced a meeting for the next morning in Boone and asked Jonathon to attend. Jack told Jonathon he had a job for him and wanted him to start immediately if he accepted.

When the meeting convened in Boone the next morning the full governing board was present along with the many interested spectators who had begun hearing rumors of the upcoming changes. To open the meeting Jack spoke of the coming weather changes which were going to force the migration to the south. He explained that he had asked Brendon to oversee the move since he had been heavily involved with the initial move to New Home. He further added that he had asked Brendon to do the preliminary work to establish a University with that task being delayed while the move south was organized and implemented. Jack then asked the board to approve the appointment of Jonathon to coordinate the movement of the Cheyenne people with that of the general population. Jonathon would report to and work closely with Brendon on this issue. All of these agenda items were approved by a voice vote of the board. Jack then took up the matter voiced by the people in the south. This involved retaining the old state names and boundaries. This was debated and was decided this was an issue which could wait until after the move south. The people in New Home far outnumbered those in the south and many of them could change their minds once they were living in a new location. A myriad of questions required answers before any movement could commence. They decided they would ask for five knowledgeable people from the south to act as advisors for relocating the various industries which had been started in New Home. Jack and Martha followed Chris home from Boone and a meeting was called for the Wolf Song people that evening. They would call it a Wolf Song supper since all of the group would be attending. Mavis was delighted as it would make the second one for that month. The group talked long into the night and stopped only to listen to the wolf lullaby which seemed to go on longer than usual. Carol commented that it was as if the animals knew they were leaving and were singing good-byes. Chris vowed he was going to record the nightly chorus for two weeks so they could take the song with them to their new home. Everyone present asked for a copy of the disc when it was completed.

Jonathon announced he was going to start his job with a poll of his people to find their preference of where they wanted to live; whether rural, small town or city. He also planned to ask them their preference of occupation and who they would like as neighbors. Chris and Brendon were going to ask for the most detailed satellite photos they could get of eastern Mississippi, all of Alabama and western Georgia. They wanted to centralize the majority of the population in one general area. Pete told the group that when Chris and Brendon went south to organize the move he would go with them. While they were busy with their tasks he would start searching for a location for the new Wolf Song community. Jack and Martha asked if they could be part of the group so they could spend their last years playing at being grandparents. Mavis thought this was a wonderful idea and asked if she and the children could start calling them Grandma and Grandpa now rather than Mr. and Mrs. Wilson.

It was past midnight when the meeting finally ended. Jack and Martha accepted an invitation to spend the night with Pete and Jackie. At breakfast the next morning Jack said he had a proposal for Pete. He told Pete that if Pete would allow Jack and Martha to accompany him on his search for new home sites for the community they might be able to point out some likely locations. In years prior to the great disaster, Jack had spent time in Montgomery on several occasions while attending to Interior

Department business. Pete was delighted to have someone familiar with the area to go along as a guide.

Soon everyone involved in the impending move was busy gathering information and studying the logistics. Public meetings were held and what little information which was available was passed on to the residents of New Home. They felt at least two years of preparation would be required before the actual move could begin.

Two years after that, in 2130, an election would be held to establish a permanent government.

Brendon, with the advice of Jack and Martha had selected a man to head the yet unnamed University. He was a sixty year old former professor of history at Harvard University named Melvin McGruder. He was given the authority to select department heads for the major fields of study.

An invitation was sent to the south for representatives to a Constitutional Convention which was to convene in August. In mid-July the group flew to Montgomery and was met by a contingent from New Home South. They quickly agreed to make Montgomery the National Capitol and to make the former state buildings the seat of the new government. The group toured Troy State University and named it as the site of the new school which as yet had no name. It was decided to try and place most of the newcomers along corridors stretching from Montgomery to Birmingham and Montgomery to Auburn. This would place most of the residents within reasonable distance of hospitals in the three cities and make communication simpler.

While all of this was taking place Jack took Pete on a tour of the city. They looked at many neighborhoods but Jack saved what he thought would be the best location for last. About ten miles north of town an old slave era mansion had been restored and made into a museum. A half mile behind the mansion stood seven modern houses. They all sat on a low bluff overlooking an impoundment of the Tallapoosa River. They sat in a shallow arc around a bend in the river. Jack had attended dinners in two of the houses. He knew that each of them contained four or five bedrooms with three baths. Each of the properties had forty or more aces fenced and all of them had horse barns and other outbuildings. As they approached the area Jack was appalled to see the old mansion was nothing but a pile of ashes with three brick chimneys pointing to the sky. They drove the curved road in front of the houses and saw no signs of habitation. They stopped at the last house where the road ended. They found the door not locked and entered to find a modern, well furnished, home covered in twenty years of accumulated dust. They also found four bodies or rather skeletons. Pete commented that Jackie and Phoebe could have the place cleaned up and livable in ten days. All of the houses were unlocked and they checked each one. Two of them contained no bodies although there were scattered bones in the yard. In one house they found a broken window with subsequent water damage from the rain which had blown in. In two of the barns they found the remains of horses which had died in their stalls. None of the cleaning would require much more than a substantial amount of elbow grease. The water damage from the broken window appeared to be minimal and could be corrected in a matter of days. Pete was anxious to show the area to Chris, Brendon and Jonathon. He suggested that Jack and Martha claim the house in the middle. It was larger than they really required but so were the other six for that matter. Jack said he would wait for the other three men to look at the arrangement before choosing.

Once the other meetings ended Pete and Jack collected the other three men and drove out to the new Wolf Song community as Pete had already started to call it. The three were as impressed as Pete had been and agreed it would meet all their needs as a community. After a few whispers from Pete, Chris and Brendon both insisted the Wilsons should take the middle house. Chris asked if anyone objected to he and Carol taking the fifth house. No one did and Brendon chose the third home which happened to be the one with the broken window and would need the most repair. It also happened to be the one with the biggest horse barn, a fact noticed by the others. Pete selected the seventh house and Jonathon the first. This left the choice of the second and sixth. Pete was sure that Melinda would insist on the house next door to Chris and Carol.

The next day the name Migration Board was selected for the group planning the move. It was approximately one thousand miles from Des Moines to Montgomery and it was determined they would use the most direct route with fuel and food depots plus charging stations every two hundred miles. The route chosen was I-80 from Des Moines to where it intersected with I-65 in Indiana. From that point they could follow I-65 all the way to Mobile. The small refinery, which had been started again in Mobile was capable of supplying all their fuel needs. A program would be started immediately to establish the required fuel, charging and food stations along the route. In two years it was thought they could keep a steady flow of people and vehicles moving over the route. Using the first satellite pictures as a guide they planned to recruit five hundred workers and put them to work rehabilitating homes, schools, churches and business places in a strip ten miles wide on both sides of I-65 from Birmingham to Montgomery. They would do the same on I-85 from Montgomery to the Georgia border. Anyone choosing to settle outside those areas would be required to do their own rehab work. Jonathon picked the I-85 from Auburn and extending across the line for ten miles into Georgia as a location for the Cheyenne people. It would provide them with ample farm and grazing land plus quick and easy access to two lakes for fishing. Chris and Brendon chose adjacent offices in the complex near the Capitol building while they were there they claimed a third office for Jonathon. Brendon commented to Chris that circumstances were certainly different than when they had met twelve years ago in Washington.

At the next day's board meeting it was pointed out that the three men in charge of the move were each going to require a secretary. They were presented with twelve young people, all of whom had the equivalent of a Bachelor's degree. After short interviews Chris chose a well-dressed young black man who impressed Chris with his self-assurance and his willingness to work on his own when Chris wasn't present. Brendon and Jonathon also selected young men who appeared bright and eager for the job. The young men were set up in the offices equipped with satellite phone and computer systems and announced they were open for business.

Chapter 8 ----- 2126

When the Wolf Song community members returned home they were informed that the Constitutional Convention was going to meet in one week. In their absence representatives had been elected in both the north and south. They had been aware of the election but supposed the convention to be some weeks away. Chris had been named as a delegate and Jack offered to take over his work with the move south until the convention was ended. The community met at Carol's invitation. They agreed to move south just as soon as they could get organized and their "must keep" possessions packed. Jack, Martha and Jonathon were told they were new but their views and opinions were critical and welcomed if they were to create a harmonious neighbor in Montgomery. They had returned home with many digital photos plus sketches of the individual properties, and one of the entire community. Mavis told Jonathon she was pleased with his choice of the house. Melinda with Brad's approval chose the house next to Chris and Carol's new home. They discussed finding a family for the remaining house but decided it was an issue which could wait. They discussed the logistics of the move and what vehicles would be required to complete it. Both Brendon and Chris were determined they were not going to turn their horses out to fend for themselves. In the end, they settled on the need for six vehicles for their convoy. First on the list was a fifteen hundred gallon fuel truck. They would need a livestock trailer capable of holding seven adult horses plus two of Brendon's milk cows, a large covered truck to carry hay, grain and water. They would also require a small furniture van for household possession plus two large passenger vans for the nine children and those people not driving. Brendon and Brad offered to look for the vehicles and Brandon vowed they would be on hand and ready for travel in no more than a month. Jack asked about Rascal and Jib. He told Chris the two mechanics were not going to be left behind when Chris moved south and besides as they would be indispensable in the event of a breakdown. They added another small truck to the list to carry the tools and personal belongings of the mechanics. They agreed to try to travel no more than two hundred miles per day. It should insure that neither the people nor the livestock would be overly stressed.

Chapter 9 ----- 2126

The Convention met in what had been the lunch room of an elementary school. The President of the Convention was a thirty-five year old high school English teacher whose name had been drawn by lottery from the list of delegate. His name was John McCleary and in a very business-like manner he called the first session of the Second Constitutional Convention to order. His opening statement was short and to the point but it would prove to be momentous. He said, "Gentlemen and Ladies, like all of you I studied government and history in school. I must confess however, that I have no idea how to go about writing the rules for a new government and I am open to suggestions. Who will be first?" Hands went in the air but in the middle of the room a man stood up and said, "I would like to be first." The voice was familiar and Chris turned his head to see Hans Wilhelm moving forward to take the microphone from John. Hans wasted little time with preliminaries, he said, "Many of you here know me as Froache the man who was called when there was a problem with predators. My actual name is Hans Wilhelm. Some of you can trace your ancestry on this continent back over four hundred years. My family came here only two years before I was born, some seventy years ago. My grandfather was an immigrant from German and I can assure you no one loved the United States more than he. He often told me that in the history of the world there had never been a more noble government document than the Constitution of the United States. It has been amended sixty-three times and it no longer fits our present situation. It will be many years before that Constitution as it now stands will apply to our present population. I am proposing that we add three more amendments and adopt that Constitution and its amendments as it existed when the world, as we knew it, ended. We will need to debate the issue and submit our final document to the people we are representing for a popular vote. Just for your information, I hold a PHD in Government and Law. I was teaching those subjects at Penn when the world ended and I hope to secure a position at our new University which today is only a dream. Thank you for your attention, Mr. President, I yield the floor back to you."

There was immediate bedlam in the room as people clamored to be recognized. When order was restored John addressed the group. He told them it appeared as if everyone present wished to address the Convention. He then told the gathering that they would use the roster of delegates and proceed alphabetically. Everyone would have four minutes to speak. They would be on a timer and after four minutes the sound system would be turned off. This process used the better part of two days. There were no alternatives offered to the proposal put forth by Hans but many insisted the Constitution be discussed and debated line by line prior to any vote to accept or reject it. Both Chris and Hans were well down on the alphabetical list and both of them agreed that the issue should be discussed at length. As is always the case, there were a few who really had nothing to say but were determined to be seen and heard.

The delegates divided into five committees to read and dissect the old Constitution and to consider proposed amendments. It took them a month of debate and in the end the Constitution was adopted with only one change. It was now the Constitution of the New United States of America. The Sixty-fourth Amendment made the term and campaign limits the law. The Sixty-fifth established seventeen as the legal age for voting and adulthood. The Sixty-sixth Amendment made it a crime and levied a two hundred dollar fine for the failure to vote in any General Election. In two years when most of the move south was completed an election would be held for President, Vice-President, twenty Senators and forty members for a House of Representatives. The Vice-President would serve as the presiding officer and voting member of the Senate in the event of a tie vote. The numbers of Congressional Members would be adjusted when a population growth of two thousand was attained.

Hans Wilhelm was elected as a President Pro-Tem to serve as an administrative officer until the election. Hans stressed to the Convention that he would not accept a nomination for any office in the coming election. He wanted to spend his remaining years teaching.

Chapter 10 ----- 2126

A week after the Convention ended a ballot was printed and delivered to every known residence in both the north and south. The following week the ballots were collected and tallied. The newly amended Constitution was approved by an astounding eight-seven percent. The U.S. was born again but it still required moving the majority of the population a thousand miles or more.

The Wolf Song group met to formulate their plans for moving. The meeting was held at the community picnic shelter with everyone attending. Jack and Martha had been invited since they were to be part of the group after the move south. Rascal and Jib had approached Chris about joining the expedition and Chris had asked them to attend the meeting as well.

The first topic of discussion was over Chris's suggestion to invite Hans Wilhelm and his wife, Chris was embarrassed to admit he didn't know her name, to take the seventh house in what was to be their enclave in Montgomery. Melinda spoke up and told the group the name was Doreen and that she had known her since she was a small child and Doreen had been a young woman in South Dakota. The discussion was short with the result being that Chris was asked to invite Hans and Doreen to join them. They settled on October 1st as a target departure date. By that time Carol's baby would be two and a half months old and should be up to the rigors of travel.

The group then took up the subject of vehicles. They finally settled on a list of seven with the first being two nine passenger vans so the nine children could ride without being cramped. Then there would be a livestock trailer capable of holding seven horses, plus two or three of Brendon's milk cows. A two thousand gallon fuel truck and a large van to carry hay, feed and water were added to the list. A furniture van for bedding and household goods was put on the list then Rascal and Jib's small tool and equipment truck. After these seven vehicles were decided Jib asked if he could make a suggestion. Jib told the group that although his body didn't reflect the habit, he like to eat, a lot. He knew where there was a food truck which was half freezer and half cooler which he thought could be rehabilitated with a minimum of work. He told them it was a big rig which would hold most of the food in their freezers, smoke houses and root cellars. Everyone agreed this was a good idea which would eliminate a pressing need to find food on arrival in Montgomery.

While they were eating BBQ ribs from the grill, Mavis who was normally exuberant in her speech and actions, shyly said she had an announcement. She then told the group she was pregnant and would be due to deliver in early April. She then added that if the baby was a boy he would be named Brendon Christopher and if it was a girl she would be named Carol Melinda. Everyone applauded and Phoebe wept openly. Phoebe said, "I get to be a grandmother and I can remember when I didn't think any of us would live long enough to have children of our own."

Two days later Carol went into labor and with both Melinda and Brad attending her in the Perry clinic, delivered a seven pound baby girl. Chris was insistent that Carol name the baby after her own mother and so Linda Ann joined the Wolf Song family.

Chris went to see his friend and former rehab construction boss Phillip. Phillip had retired and kept himself busy with a small orchard and farm near Dallas Center. It was more a large garden than small farm. He had planted forty apple trees and the rest of his ten acres in garden produce. It occupied him full time and by trading apples and produce for other necessities he lived comfortably. Phillip was not excited at the thought of resuming his old job with an even larger work force. He reasoned that on the other hand he had to move anyway so why not go early and have his choice of location. He agreed to assume his new duties on the first of December after his orchard and garden work was over for the year.

The pace became almost frantic in the Wolf Song community. Chris, Brendon, Jack Wilson and Jonathon were flying to Montgomery at least once a week. Jonathon decided his office would be better situated in Auburn and moved his operation there from Montgomery. Brad and Melinda were gathering instruments and supplies so they could open a new clinic as soon as possible after the move. Hans added another vehicle to their convoy when he announced it would be necessary to transport his law library. Phillip was placed in what had been the office of a large construction firm on the south side of Birmingham with a satellite office in Montgomery. The industries which were operating in New Home began shutting down and preparing to move to Birmingham. It had been agreed that this was the logical location for their industrial center. There were already convoys of trucks moving composite panels and structural members from Dallas Center to Montgomery. The plant had been operating at maximum production schedule since the move was announced.

The people at home in Wolf Song were making decisions which were, at times, heart-wrenching. What to take and what to leave behind were choices not easily made. Basically they were taking clothing, bedding and person items which held particular family meanings to them. Carol insisted that a small chest which had belonged to her family since the time of the Civil War must go with them as well as an old bread board which had been put together with horseshoe nails by one of Chris's ancestors in the eighteen eighties. Every family had similar heirlooms which must go with them. Pete was busy helping Rascal and Jib find and prepare the vehicles they would need. Jonathon had obtained the last three wind powered generators to come off the assembly line in Carroll before it was shut down for the move. There was a solar system in their new community but they didn't know the age or reliability of the network. The three wind machines would be more than adequate for all seven homes but it was hoped they wouldn't be needed in the immediate future. They had decided to use sleeping bags on the trip and it took until late September to locate enough for the entire group.

Rascal informed Chris that the "Ugly Bird" was finished as a flying machine. There were several cracks in the wing spars which could not be repaired and the plane could not be made safe to fly. He assured Chris that as soon as they were settled in the south he would find a replacement and have it ready to fly by spring.

In the middle of September matters became even more complicated when three teachers asked if they could go with the group. Two of them were a married couple in their mid-forties and the third was a single woman in her mid-fifties. Their primary argument for being included was that they could open a school immediately thus preventing the Wolf Song children from falling behind in their studies. The married couple owned a large van which could carry all of their belongings plus a quantity of school supplies. Phoebe instantly insisted the three teachers be included saying that educating the children was the most important task they faced. It was soon agreed that the teachers be included. This brought the number of vehicles up to ten.

By September 20, Rascal and Jib announced all of the vehicles were as well prepared as they could make them. They began loading and packing and there were many tears as cherished items were designated to be left behind. Curly and Moe had been dead for several years but Dog was still trying to be part of the action. A place was reserved for him in the back of one of the vans. One or the other of the twins would have to ride next to him. Even after ten years he refused to be separated from at least one of the twins when he wasn't sleeping.

On September 28 everything was loaded except for the livestock, the clothing they would wear on the road plus bathroom necessities.

Chapter 11 ----- 2126

By 6:00 a.m. on September 28 the little convoy was ready to roll. Brendon had spent considerable time training the animals to walk in and out of the trailer. He had mounted mangers and feed boxes in the trailer and the animals soon learned that getting into the trailer meant fresh oats and hay. Brendon had also put automatic waterers where the animals could reach them. They had decided to leave the power on in all the houses. It would increase the risk of fire but it would prevent the water pipes from freezing and in the event that anyone decided to move into any of the houses they would find them habitable. It was decided that Brendon would drive the truck pulling the livestock trailer and Rascal would drive the big refrigerator rig. The other adults would alternate with the other vehicles except Jib who would drive the truck carrying the tools and the personal possessions of himself and Rascal.

Chris was openly weeping. He was leaving a house he had helped design and build. It had been his only home for his entire adult life and it had given him comfort and shelter for those long years when he was alone. Phoebe was also in tears. She said she was leaving the only home which had been truly hers. She had put ten years of love and labor into the house and was sure she would never have another which would compare to it. Since Doreen didn't drive she was asked to ride with and supervise the younger children. The first day was uneventful. They were rolling by 6:30 a.m. on Iowa road 141. They connected with I-80 just northwest of Des Moines and from there it was a straight run east to the Mississippi River. They crossed the river and stopped at the rest area where I-80 connected with I-74. It was still early enough that Phoebe insisted they set up two portable gas grills and proceeded to prepare smoked pork chops, baked potatoes and a garden salad of greens from the refrigerator truck. Brendon unloaded the horses and cows and tied them on long ropes to trees and posts. There was even enough overgrown grass for the animals to graze. The cows were milked and the quantity didn't seem to have suffered after a day's travel. Brendon thought that would change as they traveled but not significantly. It was almost a party atmosphere as they ate supper. They slept in their own vehicles and in three motorhomes sitting on flat tires in the parking lot.

Breakfast next morning was oatmeal and toast plus apple-sauce and milk from the cooler. They were on the road by 7 a.m. Again, the day passed without incident. They crossed Illinois, turned south on I-65 and found a rest area at mile post 230. There was a large grassy area for the animals but like all such areas there was a young forest beginning to take over. One of the vans had been missing and running rough. Rascal diagnosed the problem as dirty fuel injectors. After running some solvent through the system and creating a huge cloud of smoke the engine smoothed out and began to run smoothly.

Breakfast was a repeat of the previous day and they were driving by 6:30 a.m. They saw many deer, several large flocks of turkeys and twice they saw moose standing in farm ponds apparently feeding on lily or cat tail roots.

They exited the freeway at marker 41 and drove into the little village of Uniontown. There was a small motel at the edge of town and everyone slept in a bed that night.

In the morning Phoebe, Mavis and Doreen prepared a huge breakfast of eggs, bacon, toast and hash brown potatoes. While eating, Chris couldn't help but remember his days of walking the west and having his morning meal of cold oatmeal or a stale energy bar. They drove that day to the border of Kentucky and Tennessee. It was only about 170 miles but it was their fourth day and they were all tired. There was a rest area at the state line. There was plenty of grass for the animals so they decided to stay over for a day then finish the trip over two days. They spent the evening and next day relaxing and taking short walks to loosen the leg muscles which were stiff from four days of sitting. That evening they built a bonfire with dead limbs gathered from under the surrounding trees. Chris was asked to relate some of the stories of his walks in the west. The older children wanted to hear the story of how he had acquired the three dogs which he had brought home from North Dakota. Carol was asked about her walk out of Mexico. She was reluctant to revisit those days and begged off from talking about it. Chris told the other he had a disc holding the story and would make a copy for anyone who wanted it after they were moved in and settled.

The talk then shifted to housing for Rascal, Jib and the three teachers. Jack told the group there was a small upscale housing development less than two miles from the new Wolf Song location and that he would be happy to help them find housing.

They were on the road early the next morning and now they were all beginning to be anxious to reach their destination. Chris was driving the hay and feed truck and Carol had chosen to ride with him. She had put the baby in a carrier and had it strapped to the seat between them. There hadn't been any private time for them and both of them missed their customary closeness. The morning passed quickly as they drove through the beautiful green landscape. The vehicles were in constant communication over the radios and it was decided to stop for lunch in a rest area at mile marker 22. The parking area held the usual assortment of cars, trucks and motorhomes. Chris noticed that a large van and two trucks, which were parked together, didn't show the signs of long abandonment as did the others.

As they were putting out food, from which to make sandwiches, five men walked out from behind the main building. They were rough looking with beards, long hair and dirty ragged clothing. All of them were armed. One of them carried a shotgun, one a rifle and the other three held pistols. The man with the shotgun asked who they were and what they were doing on his property. Jack Wilson replied that they were just passing through and would be on their way in less than an hour. The bearded man, while casually pointing the shotgun at the traveling group replied that they would leave when he decided to let them do so. He then pointed the shotgun at Brendon, who seemed at the point of charging the group with his bare hands, told him to sit down and face away from the gunmen. Brendon started to protest but Phoebe tugged at his arm and motioned for him to sit which he did. The bearded man then told them he was going to confiscate the livestock and refrigerator trucks and added that he was also going to keep two of the women travelers. He pointed at Mavis and told her to move over to his group. Mavis was frozen with fear and didn't budge. The gang leader then told one of his men to bring Mavis to him. As the man reached to grasp Mavis by the arm she whipped a six inch knife from behind her back and stabbed it into the side of his neck. The man dropped his pistol and staggered a few steps before collapsing. At the same instant the knife struck, the men carrying the shotgun and rifle both died from headshots from rifles. By now Chris had pulled out the little .22 colt and fired three quick rounds into the head of the fourth man as Rascal, of all people, had brought a .44 magnum out of his fanny pack and put one round into the chest of the last gunman. It all happened within five seconds and then it was quiet except for the sound of the children crying. In a few more seconds Carol and Melinda rushed into the group. Carol was carrying the old Marlin which Chris had packed so many miles and Melinda was holding a similar and equally old Winchester. Carol had stayed at the truck to change her baby's diaper. Melinda had been driving the van carrying Dog and had been searching for a leash to put on Dog so he wouldn't go exploring. She had looked up and on spotting the armed men had taken Brad's old Winchester out of the case. She slipped around the truck to where Carol was changing the baby. Explaining what she had seen to Carol the two women had crept to the front of the truck where they had a clear view of the gunmen. The men were standing on a little rise so they were visible above the travelers. There had been no signal but when the man had reached for Mavis they had both fired. The group moved the children and food to the far end of the picnic area. None of them really had an appetite. They persuaded the young ones to consume a little applesauce and milk.

They made up a batch of sandwiches for later in the afternoon and prepared to get back on the road. The question was brought up as to what they should do with the bodies. Kindly, motherly Martha vehemently snapped out, to leave them where they were, that it was as much as they deserved. As they were walking back to the vehicles the door to the main building opened and a female voice shouted, "Please don't shoot." The voice said, "We are three women and two children and we are not armed." Three tearful women and two children walked out with their hands above their heads. Brendon and Chris approached the women with their rifles at the ready. Brendon told the women to put their hands down and Chris asked them if there were any other people in the building. The woman who had led the group out of the building was he first to speak. She told Chris there was no one inside but that there were a number of weapons, primarily pistols and hunting rifles. She added that there were more guns in their van plus a large chest of stolen jewelry. She then asked if the travelers had any food they would share. The women and children had not eaten in two days and the two children were really hungry. They were directed to a picnic table where Phoebe and Martha put out ham sandwiches, applesauce, milk, and apple juice. As they ate the three women told their story.

All three of the women had been kidnapped more than two years before and held captive since then. There had been a fourth woman. She was a young black woman who had attempted to escape. She had been captured again by the gang and returned to the house where the group was staying at the time. There she was brutally whipped over a two day period then hanged from a porch post with a piece of lamp cord. The others, including the two children had been forced to watch. One of the surviving women had been caught with a pistol. She had been whipped and had her arm broken with a pool cue as an object lesson for the others. The five man gang had been operating for six or seven years looting every jewelry store, other businesses and banks to which they could gain entrance. They had a house in Columbia, Tennessee where they had stashed many millions in U.S. currency and hundreds of pounds of gold and diamonds. They were certain the U.S. would be returned to life and when that happened they would be rich and in a position to demand respect. The leader of the gang had been called Bo. The others were known as Larry, Chuck, Marv and Ricardo. The women had never heard a last name for any of the men. The woman who appeared to be the speaker for the three was named Peggy the other two were Patty and Dyan. Patty being the one whose arm had been broken and which had healed crookedly. The two girls were named Nadine and Marilyn and were Peggy's daughters. They were eight and ten years old respectively and Peggy was sure they were still alive only because Bo had said that in four or five years they would be of some use to a man. The women had been passed from man to man on a whim. To resist or try to refuse brought on another beating and being taken by force. Bo had seen the caravan pull into the parking lot and start to dismount from their vehicles. He announced they were going to select two women from the group then kill the rest. Melinda and Carol had saved a number of lives and if not all, at least several of the travelers. Peggy asked if the five of them could travel with the larger group at least until they reached a settled area. Jack told them his group was heading for Montgomery and they were welcome to travel with them. Peggy said she would like to go to Montgomery as Birmingham held too many bad memories. She told them in her old life she had been a Legal Secretary and was sure she could find work.

At this point, Hans spoke up and told her if she wanted it she had a job in his office as soon as he could have it in operation. The other two women opted to go to Montgomery and start over as well. The group discussed the rest of the trip and considered driving straight through to Montgomery. They finally decided, at Jack's suggestion, to stop at a rest area indicated on the map at Alabama mile post 299. Jack also wanted to contact the administrator for the Birmingham area and report today's events. After fueling Peggy's truck, the caravan was on the road.

Jack rode in the tool truck with Jib. He used the radio the mechanics had installed and was able to make contact with the Birmingham Administrator. This man agreed to meet the travelers where I-65 crossed I-20 on the north side of Birmingham.

Jack then made a voice recording of the day's events. They arrived at the rest area in the late afternoon and were pleased to discover it was powered by a still functioning solar array. There was water pressure and even hot water. After running the water long enough to flush the old rust colored water they were able to wash hands and faces but decided to wait until they were in Montgomery to shower or bathe.

It was late but they took the time to set up the grills, prepare steak, baked potatoes and vegetables. Carol surprised them all with four apple pies she had taken out of the freezer. Brendon contributed a large bowl of whipped cream and they dined under the soft light of the picnic area lamps and a new moon which rose in the east as the sun set in the west.

The meeting the next morning was short. It turned out the man with whom they met was one of the engineers sent to survey the composite plant in Dallas Center years ago and he knew both Chris and Jack well. He told them there had been questions when the men had disappeared years ago and the women four years later. The community did not have the manpower or resources to launch a search other than locally and he was happy to have the matter settled.

The travelers continued their journey and in early evening arrived at their new homes. Jack asked the newest members of the group to stay with he and Martha until it was decided where they were to live and housing was found for them. Pete and Jackie extended the same invitation to Rascal and Jib while Jonathon and Mavis did likewise for the three teachers. Their supper that night was again sandwiches, applesauce and milk. Mavis announced that in three days she wanted to host the first Wolf Song supper in their new home. The animals were all placed in their new homes with hay, feed and water.

The travelers spent the first night in sleeping bags but in beds that although dusty were solid and comfortable. Before going to sleep Carol mentioned to Chris that he might have to reconsider the housing they would look for. When Chris asked what she meant, Carol laughed and told him he wasn't very observant. She told him Rascal was obviously smitten with Molly, the single school teacher.

He seldom took his eyes off of her and when they were out of the vehicles he was never more than a step or two away from her. Carol said Molly appeared to reciprocate the feeling and made a point to sit by and talk to Rascal as often as she could. Carol then added that she sensed the same situation was developing with Jib and Patty. She told Chris that all four of the people they were discussing had been away from the courting scene so long they might need some help and encouragement to get the sparks flashing. She had several ideas and intended to start implementing them the next day. Before dropping off to sleep Chris thought he heard the sound of wolves howling. He sat up in bed and listened but all he could hear was Carol's gentle breathing on the other side of the bed.

Next morning the group gathered and agreed to leave their belongings in the truck until the houses were cleaned out and livable. Brendon took the male teacher and went in search of windows to replace the broken ones in the Hintz house. The teacher's name was Frank Smith who said he had experience in carpentry and construction. All of the newcomers stated they intended to stay and help with the cleaning before searching for housing for themselves. The group divided into three teams with each team taking a house and working until it was ready for a family to move in. In four days they had cleaned all seven houses including dishes, silverware, and kitchen utensils. The windows were replaced and a large trailer which Brendon had found and towed home was filled to overflowing. They had thrown out window coverings, bed clothing, deteriorated furniture and closets of clothing. The furniture truck was unloaded at the appropriate homes. The Wolf Song sign was erected on posts beside the driveway to Chris and Carol's house and the group proclaimed itself as moved in. The men spent three days looking in appliance stores within a ten mile radius. In the end they had carried home two freezers for each home and in the case of Chris and Brendon, three each. After the hay and feed truck was unloaded it was designated to carry building materials. Brendon had sketched a building and shed to become a smokehouse and wood storage facility. Frank was experienced enough to start hauling cement, bricks and the required lumber.

Chapter 12 ----- 2126-2127

Mavis had been overruled and her Wolf Song dinner had been postponed for several days. There was just too much to get done before they could all settle into their new homes. All of the homes held furniture which was in need of replacing. Not the least of their tasks was the disposal of skeletons from the houses and the scattered bones which were to be found in all the yards. It was finally decided to place them in caskets and bury them in a communal grave to be located on the grounds of the destroyed mansion. The names which were taken from papers found in the houses would be welded onto a steel plate and placed by the grave. The group brought four caskets from nearby funeral homes but the burial was delayed until more pressing tasks were completed.

Mavis announced that the Wolf Song dinner was going to be held on October 28. She conceded that since Jack and Martha had the largest house and deck, the event should be held at their home. Jonathon had shot two of the wild turkeys which were common to the area and Brendon had harvested what had appeared to be a two year old Hereford heifer. There were several varieties of frozen vegetables plus potatoes recently harvested in Iowa. Carol contributed six apple pies and Phoebe produced six pumpkin ones along with fresh whipped cream. The tables and seats were unpainted lumber put together by Brendon, Frank and the two mechanics. It was a soft, balmy evening and they all remained sitting at the table after they had finished eating. The talk centered around the future and how it would be different from the one they had known up north.

Rascal and Jib stood at the same time and Rascal said, "I have an announcement." Chris nudged Chris and said, "I told you so." Rascal then said, "You have known me for twenty years as Rascal, however I do have a real name. It is Reginald Ian MacDonald. If you don't mind I would like to be called Reggie from today on. It just doesn't seem appropriate for a fifty-eight year old married man to be called Rascal. Miss Molly Sue Brown has accepted my proposal of marriage and the event will take place as soon as we have found and rehabilitated a suitable home. Jib the floor is yours." Jib appeared to be extremely nervous but launched into his topic with no preamble. He said to the group, "I also have a real name, it is Richard Keith Jackson and I prefer to be called Richard. Miss Patricia Judith Petersen had agreed to marry me and we will be looking for a home near Reggie and Molly. Reggie and I have been partners and roommates for twenty-five years and I feel he will continue to need my guidance and counseling in whatever future lies before us. Thank you for your kind attention." Richard's short speech was followed by cheers and applause until Reggie was urged to his feet along with the two brides to be.

When the tumult ended Chris stood and addressed the group. Chris told the group he had a surprise for them but that it had to wait until it was dark. Chris then said he had a proposal for the Wolf Song group. He wanted a show of hands vote to invite Richard, Reggie and their soon to be spouses to become full voting members of the Wolf Song group. The vote to accept them was unanimous with even the children voting. Patty then stood and thanked the group for accepting them and added that she had every intention of putting some weight on Richard's skinny frame.

The conversation then turned to housing for the newcomers. Dyan, Peggy and her two daughters had decided to live together and their home needed to be within a reasonable distance of where Hans opened his law office. Jack told them he had a general idea in mind which was no more than two miles from the Wolf Song community and they would start looking the next day.

When it was fully dark and the moon was rising in the east Chris announced he was going to play a disc for them. It had been recorded at their old home in Iowa. He added that it would explain why Mavis had named their community Wolf Song. Jack and Chris went into the house where Chris inserted the disc in the stereo while Jack opened all of the windows facing the deck. The eerie, primitive sound of the wolves' serenade filled the night and all of the people sat silently as they listened. The four original women were openly weeping when, after fifteen minutes, Chris went into the house then quickly returned outside. Martha was the first to speak. She said, "It sounds so real and since Chris turned the volume down they sound farther away." Chris smiled in the darkness and told them he had not lowered the volume but had turned the disc off. What they were now hearing was live and it was not as loud because the wolves were on the ridge across the river, two miles away. Carol, Phoebe, Melinda, Jackie and Mavis stood from their seats as if by some signal and approached Jack. Jack, in some bewilderment, stood up and asked if there was a problem. Each of the women hugged and soundly kissed the old man. Melinda then spoke for all of them when she said, "Thank you for bringing us to this place. Now it truly is our new home." Jack, never at a loss for words, replied that this made the thousand mile trip well worth the effort.

There were so many tasks to be accomplished that the pace became hectic for all of them. Chris, Brendon and Jonathon went to their offices and were immediately deep in planning the logistics of the move of the people from Iowa. By way of the satellite phones they learned there had been three major blizzards since they had left the area. The storms were helping convince some of the reluctant residents that moving south might just have some merit.

Chris contacted Sven the orchardist and convinced him there was an urgent need for his service and expertise. Sven's assistant/partner had passed way the year before but there were several people whom Sven had trained who would be an asset to the southern community. Chris promised to have housing ready for Sven and Sven told him it would require a three or four bedroom house. It seems Sven had married a woman who had a twenty-five year old adopted daughter who, in turn, had two small children. Chris told him they would have a school open and functioning by the time Sven and his new family arrived.

Jonathon and Mavis drove to Auburn where they found a five room office building for Jonathon's office. Two blocks away the found a ten thousand square foot building suitable for Mavis to use for her new library.

Phillip had arrived on one of the courier planes and told them that one hundred workers had signed up for the rehab crew and, weather permitting would be on the road south within a week. They would be traveling on three buses accompanied by food and fuel trucks. They would be divided into two crews with one group working the I-85 corridor going east. The other group would work on Montgomery residential areas and then work north along I-65. The plan was to bring another three hundred workers in the spring. Jonathon suggested that Phillip move into the office he would be vacating when he moved his operation to Auburn.

Jack and the four couples who were house hunting took the vans and set out. Less than a half mile from where the Wolf Song drive entered the Jackson Ferry Road they turned off into a paved but unmarked road which after a half mile turned a corner into the pine woods. Another quarter mile brought them to a housing development which had obviously been under construction when the world ended twenty years before. There were ten or twelve homes which had been completed and landscaped. A half dozen had been lived in as was evident from cars parked in front and mail boxes on the street. The lots were spacious and the houses appeared to contain three or four bedrooms each. They began examining houses, some of which were not locked and others which required breaking a window to gain entry. The houses were similar in design and they eventually settled on four homes which took up an entire block. All four homes had fenced back yards with gates between the yards. Everything was overgrown and it would take weeks if not months of hard labor to restore the lawns and flower beds. Some of the homes contained skeletal remains but by now they were simply treated as part of the restoration process. Jack drove one of the vans back to the new Wolf Song community. The rest of the group stayed to begin the cleaning process. The next day they would return with a truck and trailer to haul away the drapes, bed clothing and furniture which was deemed unusable. The development had been built with one of the latest solar arrays which were still operating and which should provide power for many more years.

Brendon had been searching for farming and construction equipment. During his driving around the area he had discovered a long abandoned mine shaft with a rotting cover which would have to be replaced for safety with respect to children and livestock. This would be their new site for trash disposal.

Jonathon and Mavis had decided to make a temporary move to Auburn. Mavis stressed that she intended to move back to her new home before her baby was due.

Events moved at an almost frantic pace. The four men who had arrived in New Home with Jonathon called on the satellite phone to announce they would be arriving in two days. Gray Eagle had sent them to assist Jonathon in finding new homes for the Cheyenne people. They informed Jonathon that Gray Eagle was recruiting one hundred carpenters and construction workers. They would be on the road as soon as the required vehicles could be found and the convoy organized. They would make use of the facilities at Auburn University for housing and a medical clinic. There were twenty-five hundred people living in Montgomery prior to the arrival of the New Home group. A number of those people who lived on the north side of the city asked if they could send their children to the newly opened New Home school and whether they could make use of the clinic opened by the three New Home doctors.

They had opened their clinic in what had been the emergency room of a small local hospital. They were soon joined by three more doctors who had been dispensing basic medical treatment from their homes. A number of nurses inquired about positions and the little clinic soon expanded to become a ten bed hospital with an operating room for simple surgery. Brad called the semi-retired surgeon who had corrected his bad hip. The old gentleman was more than happy to become active again and flew into Montgomery, where the operating facility was expanded to two suites and became a teaching center for surgery.

Martha announced that not only was she going to be grandmother to the children of the community she was also going to become the babysitter of the group. She had the men busy removing all of the furniture from three of her five bedrooms. The furniture went to those people who were setting up homes in the new community just up the road. One room was set up as a nursery for babies and those not yet walking. The second room was to be a play room for toddlers and preschoolers. The third room was to be equipped with the required machines for video discs, audio books and the few old printed books which could be found. Martha made it known to all that she would be highly displeased if she discovered anyone in the group was hiring a babysitter.

It soon became apparent that the little house where they had opened their school was not going to be adequate for the number of children wanting to attend. Jack and Pete found the nearest school which was about three miles away from the two residential areas. From the first group of carpenters and construction workers to arrive, twenty-five of them, at Phoebe's insistence, were assigned to the rehabilitation of the school. Sven and his wife Rachel moved into a house in the new community. Rachel's daughter, Mary Lou, decided to move into a house of her own with her daughters Lori and Suzan. Lou, as she preferred to be called, said this was to enable Sven and Rachel to have some privacy and a chance to bond without having she and the children underfoot all of the time.

As the group was cleaning yet another house for Lou and her daughters the little community was given a name. The four little girls had been playing in the driveway when Julie pointed and asked, "What is that?" Dustin went to the front door and asked the adults to come and look. Standing on the front porch of a house two doors away was a pair of red foxes. The animals were probably wondering what sort of noisy creature had invaded their quiet neighborhood. The two groups watched each other for a few moments and Peggy told the girls that the animals were foxes. Finally, the animals broke and ran across the street into the tall grass and brush on the far side. Little Julie laughed and said, "See the Foxes run." Dyan, who was quiet to the point of being withdrawn following her ordeal with the men in Tennessee, surprised the group by speaking out. She said, "That would be a good name for our little enclave. Why don't we call this area Fox Run?" The group agreed and so a new place name was added to the map of Montgomery.

Chapter 13 ----- 2127

Through the winter there was a steady trickle of new people coming into the area. There were many families and individuals who felt that if they had to move again they wanted it over and done with. They managed to find the vehicles, food and fuel for the trip and headed for their new homes. It was decided that since the population would be centered around Montgomery it would make sense to have the composite plant located there rather than in Birmingham. Accordingly, the facility was dismantled and moved once again.

Brendon had scoured the surrounding area for farm machinery and in March he planted sixty acres to corn, oats and alfalfa. Brendon Jr. was now seventeen and worked alongside his father. Jr. continued working on his own when his father was busy with his other duties. The two of them had trapped more wild pigs and had a dozen young ones penned up and on their way to being domesticated. There just had not been enough room in the trucks to bring any of their swine herd south with them. They had also built an incubator and had five dozen eggs preparing to hatch.

In the middle of March Mavis returned to Wolf Song and on March 25 gave birth to identical twin girls. Carol and Melinda became curious about the number of twin births in their small community and began surveying the entire population. They discovered that twin births were more common than in the past and were increasing every year. They could only surmise that it was nature's way of rebuilding the population. They could see no other reason for the increase. In the little spare time they could manage Brendon and Jr. carved a sign for the Fox Run community and mounted it on posts at the entrance. Dyan, on seeing the sign wept and said she was in the first real home of her life. She added that she was never moving again. The twins of Mavis and Jonathon were named Margaret and Megan. They were soon called Maggie and Meggie. Martha was ecstatic over having two more babies to mother and spoil.

The school was open and in addition to the fifteen students from Wolf Song and Fox Run there were eighteen more from as far away as ten miles. Subject matter ranged from the basic ABCs to college entry level math classes. The University opened for business with one hundred twenty-five students. Many of these students were part time and more than a few situations amounted to one to one tutoring sessions.

For the past two years Brendon, Chris and their wives had been contemplating and discussing their futures. Neither man was excited about the possibility of life in public service. They had each spent ten years in one of several capacities and both wanted to return to a more private way of life. Chris had in mind to return to what had been his family's business for some 75 years. Brendon, the life-long farmer, felt drawn to some field involving agriculture. He was considering a farm seed operation in conjunction with a farm equipment manufacturing plant. They both felt that for the foreseeable future they were going to have an agrarian, rural society. The two families sat down with Jack Wilson and expressed their tentative plans. Jack was disappointed as he had seen both of them in leading positions when the new government was formed. To his credit Jack made no effort to dissuade them. He did point out the time and struggle it would take to get a viable business up and running and offered his help and advice if an when he was asked.

The two young women who had been assisting Mavis in the library took over that operation so she could be a full time mother.

With the coming of spring in 2127, the trickle of newcomers increased to a flood. The Cheyenne were the first to arrive. They came with every conceivable type of vehicle from large trucks to farm wagons pulled by horses. A few of them walked every step of the way. The construction and rehab crews worked feverishly and managed to stay ahead of that influx of new arrivals. Gardens were planted late into the summer in the hope that the warm southern climate would allow the vegetables to mature. The late arrivals would have to rely on the generosity of their neighbors for vegetables and fruit through the coming winter. Meat was not a problem as there were countless cattle, hogs and turkeys running wild. In addition the waterfowl population had exploded over the years and both ducks and geese were easy to harvest.

The winter of 2126-2127 passed and the new residents settled into their homes and farms. Their diet was limited and heavy on meat but no one suffered or went hungry.

Brendon, after much consideration, decided that rather than manufacturing new farm equipment there would be a big market for the repair and rebuilding of old equipment. He located what had been a large implement dealership and began the process of cleaning and repair of the facility to make it suitable for use as a business. He hired four men, mostly on the promise of future wages, and began to gather old equipment to be refurbished. The storage yard of the dealership was soon crowded with farm and construction equipment in various stages of disrepair. The work moved inside and Brendon felt there was enough to keep his four man crew busy all winter.

Chris drove to the new composite facility and was surprised to see the sign which had been in place for many years at the Dallas Center plant. The sign was a simple one which said Weddle Enterprises, Daniel Weddle – President. As Chris entered the lobby he was struck by a sense of déjà vu, the place seemed overly familiar. A young man was seated at a reception desk with a number of cushioned chairs arranged along two walls. The smiling young man asked if he could help. Chris told him his name and said he would like to see Lance Williams if he was available. The young man immediately pushed an intercom button and paged Lance. He told Lance there was a Mr. Weddle waiting in the office. Lance asked that Chris be shown out to the factory floor where they were setting up a press and where Lance's presence was required. Donning a hard hat and safety glasses, Chris was escorted out into the factory. It required the better part of an hour to get the machine in place and bolted down. Chris was then taken on a tour of the plant and was told the plan was to try an experimental test run in two weeks to see if the end product would meet acceptable standards. Lance then explained that they had prepared an office in anticipation of Chris returning to the plant and hoped he would find it satisfactory. They returned to the lobby and then walked down a short corridor to a small waiting room with four chairs, a coffee machine and a large video screen on the wall. A door leading off the waiting area held a sign which simply read Daniel Weddle. Chris walked through the door and was brought almost to the point of tears. He commented that the room very much resembled his father's office in Dallas Center. Lance told him it should as they had moved everything in the office and arranged it as closely as possible to the original. Even the combinations on the file cabinets and wall safe were unchanged. Lance suggested that the combinations be changed so they wouldn't have to maintain a constant guard on the room. As had been the custom of Daniel there was no lock on the door. Chris made it known that he would like to be present for the test run in two weeks and Lance assured him he would be notified the day prior to the event.

The spring of 2127 passed in a blur as the pace of new arrivals picked up. Chris, Brendon and Jonathon worked long hours getting people settled into new homes and informing them of the locations of public offices, medical and school facilities. Perhaps most importantly the meat and produce center were marked on maps for the newcomers. Seed was provided for gardens and there was a fever among the people to plant and prepare for the lean season which was sure to come. There was a steady stream of trucks moving south with the immigrants. The trucks were carrying corn and soy beans for the composite plant. They needed to stockpile enough to keep the plant operating for at least a year. The wood chipping plant was operating around the clock for the same reason.

Chapter 14 ----- 2128

Throughout the winter of 27-28 there continued to be a trickle of newcomers arriving every week. In early March word arrived that a convoy consisting of twelve people in five vehicles had been trapped in a blizzard in central Indiana. All twelve people, who included two small children, had perished in the cold. This event resulted in guards being put in place to prevent travelers from setting out in anything less than ideal weather conditions.

The Wolf Song community was a beehive of activity. A communal green house and two smokehouses had been erected and put to use. Each home now had a root cellar plus a garden plot. Brendon Sr. and Jr. had expanded the farm ground to one hundred twenty acres and were ready for spring planting.

When the word was passed that there were three single women living in Fox Run it caused a virtual stampede of would be suitors. They came with gifts of food, clothing, cars plus maintenance or repair work. It became something of a community joke whenever a strange vehicle appeared in the area. Eventually the three women chose the men they wanted and the courting frenzy came to a halt. Peggy picked a man who worked at the composite plant while Mary Lou chose a farmer. Dyan married a young man who was working with a rehab crew but was by training an EMT and planned to return to that work after all the moving was completed.

Chris tried to spend at least eight hours per week at the composite plant in addition to his duties with the moving operation. Lance Williams kept Chris informed on every aspect of the plant operation. Chris determined that when he came to the plant full time Lance must be retained as partner/superintendent. It was agreed that when the plant became a for profit operation Lance was to receive a twenty-five percent interest in the company.

Gray Eagle who was now seventy-seven years old decided it was time to turn his tribal duties over to a younger person. He announced his decision to the Cheyenne people and asked for suggestions for his replacement. He received more than three hundred nominations with a total of twenty-five names for the post. By a large majority, Jonathon was the most often named person on the list. Gray Eagle and the tribal council announced they would hold an election with the three most often named individuals being on the ballot. As had been expected, Jonathon was elected by a huge majority. His installation as Chief was carried out on the campus of the now defunct Auburn University. There was much pomp and dancing. There were many speeches and recitation of Cheyenne history. Jonathon changed his last name back to Red Wing which had been the family name until his great-grandfather had changed it to Watson, a name he had picked out of a novel he had been reading. Jonathon was also presented with a long, flowing eagle feather headdress and a red stone calumet. Both of these items were true relics dating back to the late 1800/s

Three of the young men, had driven a refrigerated truck up into Kentucky where they had harvested three buffalos. The bison meat was cooked over outdoor fires. Everyone present had at least a taste of what had been their primary food source for many years on the plains two hundred fifty years before.

It was agreed that the tribal council would be headquartered in the building Jonathon had been using as an office during the move south. The two women who had been operating the library in the absence of Mavis suggested moving the operation into the library building on the Auburn campus. It took most of three weeks for a team of volunteers to clean up twenty plus years' accumulated dust. Several windows had to be replaced and a large number of water damaged books were discarded. The library was connected to a nearby solar grid and the heating and air conditioning systems returned to operating condition. At this point a tech team, led by the renowned Jinx, moved in. They restored the computer system and trained the librarians in its use. The Cheyenne people were now in possession of the largest and most modern library existing. It was soon being used by all of the population for pleasure and perhaps more importantly for research in the arts and sciences.

The flood of newcomers continued through the summer. The numbers were about evenly divided between those choosing to live in an urban setting and those wanting a rural or small town environment. A group of about seven hundred people decided against moving to the deep south. They left the highway and settled in and around the small city of Franklin, Kentucky. Another group of about the same number settled in the outskirts of Tuscaloosa. The apparent leader and moving force of this group was a young charismatic minister. He chose the unpopulated Tuscaloosa area because, in his own words, he didn't want his flock contaminated by the ungodly who made up the majority of the population. Chris, Jack and the other leaders were uneasy about this group and their leader. It was decided that it was the choice of the people where and how they chose to live.

All of the horses belonging to Brendon and Chris were quite elderly and beginning to show it. Where they had once been sleek and round they were now showing boney spines and hips. Almost of them displayed lameness to some extent and the two men discussed what should be done for the animals. The horses were examined by a veterinarian who told them the only real problem was old age. The vet estimated that all of the animals were past thirty years of age and there was little to be done for them beyond keeping them comfortable and free of major pain. Chris and Brendon agreed to give the animals another year before deciding whether to have them humanely euthanized.

By late fall the stream of newcomers had slowed to a trickle then stopped completely. There were a few people who had refused to move again. They were told they would always be welcomed in the south if they changed their minds. It was felt that in less than fifty years the weather would prevent the growing of crops and any survivors would be forced to move.

Chapter 15 ----- 2129

There were three small newspapers in operation. One each was printed in the Birmingham, Montgomery and Mobile areas. The year, 2128, ended with the announcement that there would be a general election in April of 2129 and the first session of the new congress would convene on the first of May. Using maps of the populated areas, forty congressional districts based on a population of one thousand people were established. Some districts had more and some a few less than the one thousand. Two districts were combined to elect one senator each. Anyone interested in holding a senate or congressional seat was advised to place a notice in one of the three regional newspapers. These notices and any campaign statements would be printed free of charge. There would be time and facilities made available for public debates when needed. In several districts there were no more than one or two filings while in others there were as many as a dozen. Three men were nominated for president with Chris being one of the three. Chris didn't know who had submitted his name but suspected Jack Wilson. Chris voiced his displeasure at supper the night the nomination was printed in the Montgomery paper. To his surprise Carol approved the nomination. She pointed out that he was one of the best known men in the new U.S. He was universally respected and admired by everyone with whom he had dealt over the past twenty plus years. By the time they had finished eating the phone was ringing nonstop and the calls were all from people wishing him well in his campaign and promising support. All of the families living in Wolf Song, with the notable exception of Jack Wilson, came to the house with personal congratulations. Brendon was elated but surprised that Chris had changed his mind about running for office. After all of the well-wishers had departed Carol commented that it looked as if Chris was just about locked into the campaign. She promised to support him whatever he decided on the issue.

The next morning Chris took the newspaper with him and went to visit Jack. He asked Jack if he was responsible for the ad nominating him for office. Jack immediately answered yes and asked for a chance to explain why. Jack said it was simple. The office called for a man whom the people knew and could trust and follow. Chris, Jack said, met those standards better than anyone in the country and duty demanded that he accept the responsibility. Martha even entered the discussion by telling Chris that the babies and children she was tending were dependent on someone to get the new nation off to a good start and that he was the best qualified person she knew. With that said, Martha patted Chris on the back and with a smile returned to tending her babies.

Chris went home and spent the remainder of the morning with Carol discussing what their future would hold if he became president and served the two allowed terms. It would mean that he would be unable to return to the family business for another six years. There would be less time for the family for the same period which could be a problem with the three older kids going through their teen years. Carol pointed out that with the capital being in Montgomery they could stay in their home and he could be home every night when he wasn't out of town.

That afternoon Chris drove to the composite plant and huddled with Lance for two hours. They settled on a plan which made Lance the company president with full authority for the entire operation, the only restriction being that no part or share of the business could be sold without approval of Chris and Carol.

Chris returned home and told Carol it appeared as if it was now official that he was a candidate for the presidency of the New United States. He called Jack to confirm it with him. Jack's response was that he had known Chris would see his duty and do the right thing.

Over the next few days Chris spent a lot of time at his desk composing a statement for the newspapers. It was finally condensed to simply stating what he would ask the new congress to enact into law. First on the list was a monetary system with new currency and coinage. He felt it was time to move on from the bartering system which they had been using for over twenty years. There was also a need for a police force and small penal system plus an agricultural department. He planned to appoint people to head those endeavors and would ask the senate to confirm the appointments. As there were no organized political parties he would ask permission to name his vice-president as it needed to be someone with whom he could work closely and harmoniously. Chris printed his statement and sent copies to the three newspapers where they were printed along with a request for comments from the voters. The other two candidates were a former school teacher and an attorney. Neither of the two voiced any demands for a public debate so Chris refrained from doing so as well.

When the ballots were printed and delivered to the districts the entire area was given a shock. The group in Tuscaloosa refused to accept the ballots and returned them with a curt note. The note simply stated that the people of Tuscaloosa did not consider themselves as citizens of the New United States. The note went on to say that the Tuscaloosans did not and would not recognize any authority outside their own established boundaries.

Three men were sent to determine what was happening in Tuscaloosa. At milepost seventy six on the east side of the city they found the highway barricaded and four armed men guarding the road block. They were told that visitors were not welcome and they should tell their ungodly superiors to leave the true believers alone. This information was a shock to everyone in Montgomery and the rest of the U.S. It was decided that no action would be taken in respect to the situation until the new government was formed and in place.

There were several very heated public debates among the senatorial and representative candidates. Chris held a number of open public forums at which citizens were encouraged to ask questions on any subject pertinent to his qualifications for the office of president. Over the course of these forums Chris basically retold his life history several times. He was asked over and over again about the two men he had shot and killed. Each time he replied that the lives of his family and himself had been threatened. If the situation were to be repeated he would do the same thing again.

Chapter 16 ----- 2129

April came and with it the election. To no one's surprise Chris was elected by a huge majority and he and the others elected began the task of organizing a government. Chris, at the urging of Hans Wilhelm asked John McCleary to consider being the new Vice-President. The government, for the foreseeable future, was going to operate from the buildings on what had been the campus of Troy State University. It was felt the buildings would be adequate to their purpose for many years to come.

On the first of May the Senators and Representatives swore themselves into office by reciting the old Pledge of Allegiance with the only change being the insertion of the word "New" in front of United States. Chris then addressed the group and asked them to confirm Hans Wilhelm as the Chief Justice of the Supreme Court. This was a surprise to Hans who could only gape in wonder as the Senate voted unanimously to put him in the Chief Justice chair. After this was accomplished Hans in turn swore Chris and John into their offices using the old oath which had been in place for many years. This concluded the first day of the New U.S.

Carol had invited all of the Wolf Song people to a potluck supper that evening. When Brendon and his family arrived Brendon nodded at Chris and said, "Good evening Mr. President", with a mischievous grin. Chris returned the gesture and replied with, "Good evening Mr. Secretary." Carol, who had been told of the plan Chris had for Brendon, smiled and added, "Congratulations Brendon." Brendon asked what was going on. Chris told him the country needed a Secretary of Agriculture and the President didn't know anyone better qualified than Brendon

Hintz. Brendon protested that he didn't have the education for such a post. Chris reminded him of the time several years ago when Mavis had declared that, "Her daddy knew more about farming than anybody." Brendon hadn't denied it then and now it was too late to do so.

The next month was incredibly busy. The Congress was scheduled for three sessions per year. They would convene in January, May and September with each session slated to last for the month it was convened but could be extended by a simple majority vote. With Chris being the administrator of the Executive Branch he wanted people in place so the government could begin to function immediately. He settled on six departments which were: Education, Interior, Agriculture, Treasury, Military Affairs and Health. Chris spent hours on the phone and driving, asking people he knew and trusted for recommendations of people to fill the posts. He finally settled on six highly qualified people to fill the offices. Of the six, three were women who were all highly qualified and eager to participate in the new government. These three were to fill the offices in Health, Interior and Education. The Military Secretary was to be filled by a man whom Pete had told him about. Patrick Cofer was a West Point graduate and at the time of the great catastrophe had been the youngest Brigadier General in the Army in the past two hundred years. The Attorney General and Treasury Secretaries were men esteemed by their colleagues and Chris felt there would be little opposition to the confirmation of any of the six. The only real debate was over the confirmation of General Cofer. There were minority groups in both the House and Senate who argued there was no reason for a military presence in such a small community. When it was pointed out that the military was also going to act as the local police, until there was a substantial population growth, the nomination was approved.

Chris had decided he wanted to add a new, temporary department to his government. It was to be called the Department of Exploration. The little ship Discovery had been refitted and had been sitting in a dry dock for over a year waiting for a new mission. Three guns had been mounted on her fore and aft decks.

On her previous ten year cruise she had been fired upon by shore batteries from the coasts of both China and New Zealand. The crew had no option except to retreat at full speed. All of the former crew had vowed never to sail on her again unless she was armed. Chris had in mind to send the ship on a year's long voyage to explore the coast of Central and South America. Following that he envisioned a two year cruise to the west coast of Africa, the Mediterranean basin and the coast of Europe. Chris also wanted to send a six scout teams of five or six men each to explore the eastern half of the former U.S. to see if there were any pockets of survivors still existing. Congress quickly accepted this idea and Mike Dunbar was sworn in as the Secretary of Exploration.

Chris was uncertain about the extent of his powers as President. To be on the safe side of any controversy over those powers he asked the congress for advice and consent for his first two endeavors.

First he asked for the organization of a corp. of exploration. He wanted the Discovery equipped, manned and provisioned for a year-long survey of the east coasts of Central and South America. He also asked that the Corps of Exploration, made up of individuals who were eighteen to forty years of age be started on a training regimen with the goal of setting out on March 1, 2130. Their goal would be to explore the eastern half of the old U.S. in an effort to ascertain whether there were individuals or pockets of survivors anywhere in the former Eastern U.S. He wanted to start with forty trainees with a final goal of six teams of five people each. There were sure to be individuals who would drop out of the program or became ill or injured and unable to continue. He asked that at least two women be included on each team and at least one person per team with basic medical training and experience.

The second operation was much larger and would involve hundreds, if not thousands of people. He proposed a system of coinage and currency which would move them away from the current barter system and put their economy on a cash basis. He proposed that a convoy be sent north to Fort Knox where an entry, by whatever means, would be made into the gold and silver repositories. The mints and currency printing plants would be dismantled and moved to Montgomery along with all stocks of currency paper available. The largest bank in the city of Montgomery was to be converted to a new precious metals repository and at least twenty banks were to be opened in the three major cities. The value of gold would be settled at one hundred dollars per ounce and silver at ten. No coins would be minted with a value less than ten cents or currency printed of less than five dollars. Anyone convicted of counterfeiting would be banned for two years to at least five hundred miles west of the Mississippi River. A second offense was a three year ban and a third would be a lifetime ban. When the coining and currency printing had produced enough cash every adult living within the boundaries of the New U.S. was to be given ten thousand dollars in cash. They would be encouraged to make use of the newly established banks. Prices on goods and services would have to be negotiated by the individuals who were involved. The goal was to move five hundred tons of gold and an equal amount of silver to Montgomery with the possibility of moving more at a later date.

Congress, being limited by rule to meeting only for the month of April went to work immediately on the proposals put forth by the President. Committees were formed, debates held and by the first of February trucks, tools and "experts" were being gathered at marshaling yards in Birmingham and Montgomery. Work was started on all of the bank buildings which were to be utilized under the plan. A training facility was set up on the campus of Alabama State U. and recruitment began for candidates of the Exploration Corps.

Chapter 17 ----- 2130

While the progress of government was moving along nicely the mood in the Wolf Song community took a downturn. At the February Wolf Song dinner, Mavis announced that she and Jonathon needed to move out. With Jonathon newly installed as Chief of the Cheyenne they both felt it was important that they live in the center of the Cheyenne population area.

In late February, Brendon Jr., who was now twenty announced that he was going to marry the young woman he had been dating. He had proposed, she had accepted and both of them wanted to proceed immediately. On hearing the announcement, Mavis immediately suggested that the newly married couple move into the house she and Jonathon would be vacating. Phoebe was quick to second this suggestion. It would negate the chance of someone new moving into the community, but more importantly it would keep one of her "babies" closer to home.

As winter began to turn to spring the condition of the Belgians and Percherons continued to deteriorate. Chris and Brendon discussed the situation and determined they would not allow the animals to suffer any longer. Brendon used a small dozer and backhoe to excavate an eight foot deep trench long enough to hold the five work animals plus Phoebe's black riding mare. A veterinarian was called to euthanize the animals. This was accomplished by administering a lethal dose of drugs which simply stopped the heart and was painless to the horses. They were placed beside a small grove of Poplar and Hickory trees under which the horses had sought the shade on hot summer days. The two men talked of erecting a marker over the grove but settled for planting two rows of trees along the length of the ditch.

Brendon was determined to find a pair of horses for another team while Chris, who had been more emotionally involved with his horses, decided he didn't want another team.

The oldest of the children had progressed through the material offered at the new public school and were all taking college intro courses. It was agreed they should enroll at the new American University on the old Troy State campus. A small bus was rehabilitated and with Chris Jr. as the designated driver began making the daily six or seven mile trip to the campus. Most of the children wanted to study some form of Engineering except Kathie and Pearl who wanted to study medicine and follow in the footsteps of their mothers.

At the age of forty-six both Molly and Patty were pregnant as were Peggy and Dyan. At age sixty-two Reggie was shocked at the prospect of becoming a father. At the same time he was giddy with delight. He became so solicitous of Molly's welfare she accused him of trying to smother her with attention.

In September the legislature met for the second time. Chris submitted two more names for Supreme Court Justices. He also proposed establishing five district courts and added people to fill those seats. The Senate quickly approved those nominations and moved on to the most pressing issue they faced, how to pay for government. The answer, of course, was taxation. They debated for the entire month without reaching the answer. Two committees were formed which would meet after the session ended. Their goal was to have several plans ready to submit to Congress during the January session.

Chapter 18 ----- 2131

The first order of business for Congress for 2130 was to extend their sessions to three sixty day meetings per year. They also established a salary rate of ten dollars for every day they were in attendance. No exceptions were to be granted except for the death of an immediate family member. This law was immediately challenged as unconstitutional. The case was submitted to the Supreme Court.

The Court, with nothing else on the calendar, heard the testimony and in a matter of two days ruled that the act was legal and binding. The Court pointed out that Congress must have the power and authority to act on many issues if the country was to have a viable, working government.

A tax bill was debated and passed to become effective in 2131. It levied a flat four percent tax on all net income and all profits from any business transactions. After five years there was to be a tax levied on all real estate with the rate of taxation to be determined at a later date.

The Treasury Department, with the consent of Congress, published a list of currency and coinage values. The money would be backed by the value of the gold and silver held in the repository. Currency would be in denominations of five hundred, one hundred, fifty, twenty, ten and five dollars. Coinage in gold would be fifty, twenty-five and one dollar. The silver coins would be minted with values of ten, five and one dollar. Smaller coins of an alloy yet to be determined would be valued at fifty, twenty-five and ten cents.

On March 1 the convoys of vehicles bound for Fort Knox began to set out. They were divided into units of ten vehicles which would leave a day apart. They would make use of the fuel and food stations which had been established for the move south. It would require a steady stream of supply vehicles to keep those stations replenished.

The exploration group had finished training and the teams were ready to set out. The group had been renamed the Corps of Discovery in honor of the Lewis and Clark expedition of three hundred years earlier. There were five teams of six members each with two women and a medic on each team. There were an additional five men who had completed training. It was decided that rather than waste the time and effort invested in their training they would form a five man team and be sent to the west to explore Mississippi, Louisiana and east Texas.

Each team carried two satellite radios and each member was armed with a light pistol and a medium caliber hunting rifle. The teams would live off of the land which meant a meat heavy diet. Each team member would carry a year-long supply of multi-vitamins to supplement their diet. Each team would also carry a supply of flyers on water proof paper. The flyers were to be posted in a prominent place wherever they found indications of people but were unable to make contact. The flyer would explain their mission, where they were based and invite any readers to make the trek to Montgomery to join them.

The Discovery was made ready to sail. The skipper was the former First Mate from the previous voyage. This time, there was a crew of fifty men and women with fifteen of the first crew on board. With human nature being what it was, all crew members were required to submit to inoculations which would render them sterile for a period of eighteen months. The same regulation was applied to the Corps of Discovery members.

The Discovery teams were numbered one through six. The team number was to be the radio call sign for each team. The teams would primarily follow the Interstate highway routes with side trips as they saw fit and had the time. Team One was tasked with exploring the Gulf Coast, Florida, Georgia, and

South Carolina. Team Two would cover northern Georgia, North Carolina and eastern Tennessee. Team Three was assigned a route through eastern Kentucky, Virginia, West Virginia and southern Ohio. Team Four had the longest route which would take them through the north Atlantic states including New England and Maine with their return to be through upper New York and western Pennsylvania. Team Five was tasked with covering western Ohio, Michigan and if possible Wisconsin. It was doubtful whether Team Four could complete their trek before winter and they were advised to find a place with heat and a food supply no later than October 15, then wait out the winter in as much comfort as possible.

On March 3 the convoys of trucks headed north towards Kentucky. The two scout teams heading north and east hitched rides with the trucks as far as Fort Knox and would proceed on foot from there. Teams Two and Three rode to Auburn before starting their walk. Team Six was driven to Mobile where they started walking west along the Gulf Coast.

In a matter of two weeks all of the vehicles had arrived at Fort Knox. Two barracks at the nearby Army base had been cleaned out and the men were housed in reasonable comfort. A dining hall was also put back in working order so regular meals could be served.

The men assigned to the actual break-in of the bullion storage areas were outfitted in bio-hazard suits and the assault commenced. The suits were used on the chance that storage areas were booby trapped with poison gas of some type. Essentially, they cut their way in using both electric and gas torches. In less than a week they were standing in the vaults looking at untold millions worth of gold and silver.

At the same time, the nearby mint and printing plants were being taken apart and loaded on trucks for transport to Montgomery. At ten tons per truck it would require a total of one hundred loads to transport the bullion to Montgomery. With only twenty trucks available it was obvious that moving the gold and silver would take all spring and early summer. Dismantling, moving and reassembling the mint and printing plant would take even longer. There would be no new coinage or currency before late winter or early spring. It was felt there was little chance of a robbery attempt on the bullion trucks. To be on the safe side however a number of light armored vehicles were obtained from the nearby Armored Division Base and thoroughly rehabilitated. One of these vehicles with five heavily armed men would escort every two of the bullion carrying trucks. There was soon a steady, if scant, number of trucks moving south to Montgomery.

The empty trucks were loaded with food, clothing and a variety of other goods then sent north again. The trucks resupplying the fuel stations were busiest of all. In May, the Congress and Treasury Department conferred and decided to move another one hundred tons of both gold and silver which meant one more trip for each of the bullion trucks. By June the bullion had been moved and the repository at Fort Knox had been sealed by welding three quarter inch steel plates over all the doors. An alarm system was rigged to radio a signal to Montgomery if entry was attempted. There were just not enough people to spare for a permanent guard force. The machinery from the mint and printing plant was being moved one piece at a time and then reassembled in Montgomery The target date for completion of that operation was early December but no one was confident of completing the task on time.

Joel M. Coffer who was the newly appointed Secretary for Military Affairs had gone to Fort Knox and with a small crew restored three medium tanks and twenty armored infantry vehicles. They were all brand new but had been sitting idle for twenty-four years. The infantry vehicles which rode on eight solid rubber tires were driven to Montgomery while the tanks were loaded on trailers and hauled back to the Capital.

Chapter 19 ----- 2131

Reggie and Richard had been prowling all the airports within driving distance of Montgomery. They were determined to find a plane for Chris to replace the Ugly Bird. They had examined many planes but had not found one which suited them. Someone finally suggested they take a look at the old Naval Air Station at Pensacola, Florida. The two men took their old, fully loaded, tool truck and made the two hundred plus mile drive to Pensacola. There they found dozens of training planes and many war planes. On the civilian side of the field were many aircraft but twenty-four years of exposure to the salt air had left them in sad shape. They began going into the hangars lining the strip. Finally, in a building identified by a badly faded sign as having belonged to a long gone shipping company they found what they were seeking. Sitting up on jacks with the landing gear extended was a twin engine, late model jet. They climbed inside and saw it had seating for ten passengers plus a small conference table. In the rear was a roomy cargo and luggage storage area. In addition, there was a small galley and bathroom which included a tiny shower. Piled on seats in the cabin were a number of books and maintenance manuals which indicated that the plane was new or nearly so. Both of them had worked on similar aircraft so the task of rehabilitating this one was not the least bit daunting to them.

They drove back to Mobile where they left their truck and borrowed a car for the return trip to Montgomery. On reaching home they swore Molly and Patty to secrecy then explained what they doing. They then asked if it would be possible for the women to manage if they were gone for four or five weeks with the promise it would be the last extended trip they would make.

The women agreed as Patty winked and told Richard he would have time to make up when he came home.

Rascal and Jib, as they still called each other, loaded the car with clothing, non-perishable food and headed south again. In Mobile they swapped the car for their truck and were told a tanker truck would be dispatched to Pensacola with the proper fuel when they called for it.

Rascal and Jib began by cleaning the cockpit area, using a powerful vacuum, then damp cloths. They drained all of the liquids from the various systems including fuel then purged the lines and replaced the various liquids. The charged the batteries and replaced two of them which would not indicate a full charge after a week. Using battery power they cycled the landing gear several times to insure it was working properly. Several seals which had deteriorated over the years were replaced and they decided it was time to check the engines. Using their truck they towed the plane out to a wash stand and scrubbed it top to bottom. A call to Mobile brought a fuel truck with enough fuel for several test flights and the hop to Montgomery. When they first turned power on to the instrument panel they had noticed the hour meters for both engines indicated only fifteen hours so they were convinced they had a brand new airplane. Both engines started with a minimum of turning then, with the wheels chocked and brakes locked, Rascal pronounced the plane ready to present to the President but Jib said it was lacking something. On both sides of the nose, in bold block letters he painted, UGLY BIRD II. Below the lettering he painted the scruffy looking bird just as it had appeared on the original. Now they needed to find a pilot to ferry the plane to Montgomery. They considered several men including Brandon but finally decided they would ask Pete Brown. Pete had undergone experimental eye surgery performed by a young surgeon who had some radical theories with regard to treating vision problems. The surgery had dramatically improved Pete's vision and he was flying again. When the two mechanics returned home they immediately went to Pete and explained their plan then asked him to fly the plane to Montgomery. Pete readily agreed. He had no reservations about flying a plane pronounced to be airworthy by these two men. Pete taxied and ground tested the airplane then took off and flew to Montgomery. He landed at the old Maxwell AFB which was being used by two companies as home for their flight operations. The plane was placed in a medium sized hangar on which the two mechanics had hung a sign announcing that it was now the home of "The Oily Rag Aircraft Repair and Restoration Company."

It was now late July and the monthly Wolf Song supper was only two days away. The people living in the Fox Run community were now included in the supper and it had become a potluck affair. By unanimous consent the meal always included ham from Brendon's smokehouse. It had become a rather large gathering and was always held at the home of Jack and Martha Wilson. Tables and benches were set up in the yard, or if the weather was inclement, there was room for all of them on the covered deck. All of the adults except Chris had been told secretly about the new plane. During the after supper chatting; the two mechanics had announced that they were opening a repair business. They invited Chris to come look at their new building and give them his opinion on their choice of location and facilities. As an "after thought" Rascal invited the entire group to come at ten A.M. in two days. He promised milk and cookies for everyone who came. Tea and coffee supplies had been exhausted years before so those drinks were no longer an option.

At the appointed hour, almost everyone from both communities had gathered in the lobby and office of the hangar. As promised, there was milk and cookies set out and the children were making the most of the situation. The adults commented that the only thing missing was coffee or perhaps tea. Molly and Patty had baked for two days to insure there would be plenty plus enough extra that each family could take some home. Finally, Chris was invited to walk out into the hangar to inspect the work space. Chris glanced at the plane then told the mechanics he was happy to see they already had work. Jib smiled and told him that job was already completed and he wanted Chris to look at the work they had done on the nose of the plane. It finally registered with Chris what was painted on the nose. He turned to the men and asked what was going on. Rascal put his hand on Chris' shoulder and said, "Boss, we talked about it and decided you were never meant to be without your own plane. The only thing in question was whether that "Ugly Bird" should be on the President's personal plane. If you don't like it we can remove it. Other than that the bird is fueled and ready to fly anywhere within forty-five hundred miles. It is yours and while there is no ignition key, here is one for the cabin door." At this point, Pete joined the three men and noticing a quivering lip and a tear beginning to form he slapped Chris on the back and said, "Get a grip on it, Presidents don't cry in front of their constituents." After Chris had inspected the aircraft inside and out the rest of the group were invited to go onboard and examine the plane. After Molly and Patty had completed their tour they huddled together for a couple of moments then motioned for Rascal and Jib to join them. The two men were told if they would remove the seats from the plane interior the women would give the plane interior and the seats a proper cleaning. They said they didn't want Chris to be embarrassed by having to ask people to fly in less than a spotless airplane. Pete asked Chris if he would fly him to Perry. He wanted to see if the twin jet they had abandoned when they moved south could be restored to a reliable condition. It would mean taking Jib and Rascal along to do the work and this of course would depend on getting permission from Molly and Patty.

Chapter 20 ----- 2131

Before the Perry flight could be planned Chris was faced with his first crisis as President. For some time rumors had been filtering out of the settlement in Tuscaloosa. There was very little direct communication with the outside world but notes were passed and secrets were whispered whenever contact was made. It was said that the young evangelist who had led them away from the main body of citizens was taking more and more control of their daily lives. No marriages were allowed except with his approval. Attendance at religious services was required twice daily. The new rules were vigorously enforced by a troop of armed men and women who were all devoted followers of the new messiah as he had begun to call himself. Investigators sent from Birmingham were turned away outside of Tuscaloosa by armed guards who warned them not to return. Eventually, three young couples who wanted to marry but were forbidden to do so because the "messiah" had not approved the young women, escaped. They eluded the guards and by using back roads and traveling through the fields and woods made their way to Birmingham. The six young people not only had their personal experiences to relate they had several hours of recordings which they had secretly made. They had recorded speeches made by the self-proclaimed "messiah", exchanges with members of the guard force and casual talks with other citizens. The "messiah" was clearly heard to say that God had spoken to him, had anointed him as the Son of God and the only route to heaven was through his blessing and the granting of his every wish. Every young woman who wanted to marry was required to spend a week in his bed before she was approved.

Any man having sex with a woman who had not been approved was subject to a number of punishments up to and including death. Two young men were known to have been castrated then garroted. Women had been publicly whipped and branded on the arm with a large "W" indicating whore. They were forbidden to wear long sleeved garments to conceal the brand. It was also made clear that any man who contributed enough gold or silver, usually in the form of jewelry, could marry any single woman he desired. Young women of thirteen and fourteen were thus forced into a life of virtual slavery, often involving men of the guard force. The interviews with the escapees had been recorded. These recordings along with those brought by the young people were immediately sent to Montgomery. One of the young couples went along as well.

The recordings and the young couple were presented to Chris. After listening to a half hour of the discs and talking with the couple, Patrick Richardson and Melissa Johansen, Chris got on the phone and called his Military Affairs Secretary, Joel M. Cofer, the Attorney General, Bill Weston and Jack Wilson, the man whose advice he most trusted. Chris briefly explained the situation then played all of the recordings. The three men asked questions of Patrick and Melissa who were then excused. When the four government men were alone Chris turned to his advisors and asked for their recommendations. Bill spoke first, he said, "These people, or at least the leader, do not recognize the authority of this government. However, they were assisted in their move here and reside within the area claimed by this government. In my opinion they are subject to our laws and the penalties for ignoring those laws. Before acting I suggest we have the Supreme Court listen to the tapes and rule on our authority to take action." Jack Wilson spoke and agreed with Bill. Chris immediately called the three justices and asked whether it was possible to come to his office, immediately if possible. All three agreed and soon appeared. They were apprised of the situation, given the recordings to listen to and asked to render an opinion on the government's right to intervene. It was stressed that time was of the essence. The justices took the recordings and written statements and retired to their chambers while promising their opinion by the next morning.

Chris then asked Joel if he could provide a military or police force if the situation developed to the point where such a force was called for. Joel surprised them by saying he could field two hundred men within two days. It turned out that many of the young men had been enamored by the tanks and APCs brought back from Fort Knox. The men had besieged Joel's office begging to be allowed to train with the machines. As a result Joel had three well trained tank crews plus almost two hundred men with basic infantry training. They did not yet have uniforms but all could be outfitted with helmets and flak jackets.

The next morning a written message from the court was delivered to the President. The message stated that not only did the President have the right to intervene in Tuscaloosa he was obligated to do so for the protection of American citizens. A phone call to Joel assured Chris that the Militia would be prepared to move out by seven a.m. the next day.

For the first seventy-five miles the tanks were loaded on the same trailers which had brought them to Montgomery. Joel had called in a fifty-five year old Army veteran and appointed him to the rank of Major. Interestingly, it was the same rank he had held at the age of thirty-one when the Army ceased to exist. He was to command Company A of the new U.S. Army. Joel selected two men in their mid-thirties to command two platoons of fifty men each and commissioned the as First Lieutenants. One man in each vehicle was given the rank of Staff Sergeant and was nominally in charge of that squad. Every man was warned not to fire his weapon until told to do so or was being fired upon by others. The three officers, accompanied by Joel, rode in a staff car equipped with a siren and loud speaker. The convoy left promptly at seven. They covered seventy-five miles in a little over two hours. The tanks were unloaded, the turbines fired up and they proceeded on toward Tuscaloosa. In the lead was the staff car, followed by the two tanks and then the ten APCs.

On the outskirts of Tuscaloosa the convoy approached the expected road block. It was a rather flimsy barricade of wooden poles with two vans parked behind it. There were six heavily armed men standing behind the barricade. On reaching the barricade the two tanks spread out to the extreme edges of the road with the staff car and one APC parked between them. Major Benson exited the staff car and ten men from the APC lined up behind him. Major Benson then addressed the guards at the barricade. He said, "We are here under direct orders from the President of the United States. We do not wish open conflict but if you so much as point a weapon at us my men will open fire on you. My advice is for you to put your weapons on the ground, get in your vehicles and return to your headquarters. We will give you one hour to assemble your leaders and inform them we are coming. Please emphasize that we do not wish open conflict but we will react with full force if we are fired upon. While you dismantle the barricade we are going to search your vehicles for any additional arms or explosives. You have ten minutes beginning right now; then we will move on you." The six thoroughly cowed guards all placed their weapons on the ground and began to remove the barricade. Ten men from a second APC were waved forward and told to search the two vans. They discovered two light machine guns and several pounds of plastic explosives. The militia members spent the hour promised to the guards by eating their prepared lunches and exercising leg muscles, cramped from three hours in the close confines of an APC. When the hour had expired the troops mounted up and drove directly to what had been the campus of the University of Alabama. They had been told that the new "messiah" had moved into the home of the former President of the University and very seldom left the premises. Driving over the overgrown lawn which was on the verge of becoming a young forest, the two tanks faced the house at point blank range. The ten APCs formed a half circle around the tanks with alternate vehicles facing in and out. A crowd had begun to gather and after twenty minutes Joel estimated there were at least five hundred people silently watching. This constituted the majority of the population. At this point Major Benson, using the loudspeaker, addressed the house. He said, "Mr. Grundy please come out of the house. We mean you no physical harm but this community is now under Martial Law and any resistance will be met with force. We are here by order of the President and we mean to carry out the commands given to us." Turning the speaker toward the crowd he assured them no one was in danger as long as they did not become involved. Suddenly the front door opened and a number of people rushed out. Leading the way was a tall man with a tangled mass of unruly hair and matching beard. He was clad in a soiled robe and sandals. On his head was a small golden crown. He was also carrying an automatic assault rifle. Close behind the first man were two others similarly dressed but minus the gold crown. These two were followed by perhaps twenty-five men who were all heavily armed. The man with the crown began screaming. He was waving the rifle over his head as he shouted, "How do you dare call me by that name in front of my people? I am the Christ, the Messiah. This is Holy ground and you infidels area defiling it. I demand that you leave at once or there will be war." As if to emphasize his last remark he brought the rifle to his shoulder and fired one round at the turret of the nearest tank. The gunners in the two nearest APCs instantly fired a three round burst each from their twenty mm guns. From forty feet away their aim was true and the six heavy slugs cut the man almost in half. The rounds also struck and killed the other two men dressed in robes plus four of the guards standing in a group behind the leaders. It was suddenly very quiet except for the idling engines of the militia vehicles. Major Benson told the remaining guards to slowly place their weapons on the floor and step away from them. By the time that move was completed it became apparent there was a fire inside the house. One of the guards informed Major Benson a small supply of vehicle fuel was stored in the back of the house. Another guard told them three young women were chained in second floor bedrooms. In less than a minute two crews of three men each had retrieved bolt cutters from the APCs and ran into the house. Minutes later the men reappeared shepherding three young women plus two older women who had been cowering in the kitchen. The three young women had been naked but had been given shirts by the militia. The shirts barely covered them but it was better than nothing.

The women were placed in the back of an APC and all of the vehicles were pulled back from the burning house.

Joel got on the loudspeaker and announced; any citizen who wished to file a complaint or make a comment would be welcomed and each would be heard and their comments recorded. There was not much to do except watch the old house burn to the ground. The weapons on the veranda had been picked up and stored in an APC but the bodies were left where they lay. It was the general feeling of the militia that being burned in the house fire and then being left to the elements was as much as these particular dead men deserved. While the fire was burning three middle aged women approached the militia member who was standing guard in the vicinity of the APC where the three young women were resting. He happened to be one of the new Staff Sergeants appointed the night before and took his new responsibility seriously. He held up a hand to stop the women and said, Ladies I don't think you should be in this area. There are at least twenty-five of those guardsmen not accounted for and we don't know what they may attempt." The three women stopped and one of them told him not to worry about the missing guards. She told him that when word was spread that the US Army was approaching they had loaded back packs and headed northwest towards Columbus, Mississippi. She added that tomorrow she would present the army with names and photographs of every man and woman in the guard unit. She then told him that the three women were the mothers of the three young women one of which was not yet seventeen years old. She finished by saying, "Right now those girls need their mothers and clothing more than they need an armed guard." The sergeant waved them on then stopped them again and said, "Ma'am if you come to make a statement tomorrow as for Sergeant Brill, I'm sure the Major and Mr. Cofer will want to hear you stories personally."

Statements from complainants and their corroborating witnesses lasted for more than six days. Every word was recorded. The recordings would be transcribed to paper in Montgomery and the transcriptions provided to each attorney assigned to prosecute or defend the accused. It would require the services of the majority of the attorneys practicing in the area. The government promised every lawyer involved a flat four hundred dollar fee when the new currency became available.

A total of twenty-seven people were arrested with eight of them being women. They were held in the Montgomery city jail which had been cleaned up and somewhat refurbished. Security was not extreme but the prisoners were informed that any attempt to escape or an assault on guards or other prisoners would result in their eventual sentence being doubled.

The residents of the Tuscaloosa area were urged to move to the Montgomery area and there was immediate agreement although a few chose to move to Birmingham and a number of others selected Mobile as their destination.

Most of the accused, in an apparent hope of clemency, pleaded guilty. They had been accused of simple theft and intimidation by threat of force. They were sentenced to shunning for terms of six months to one year. They were required to spend all of their time within their respective residences and could speak to no one except their immediate families if any such resided with them. Five other were banned for a period of three years. Two of these five were women who had been instrumental in the public whipping and branding of women accused of having sex not approved by David Grundy. In two instances they had rubbed salt into the fresh lash marks and brands. The last man was convicted of beating then sexually assaulting a seventeen year old girl who resisted his advances. He then threatened to kill her if she made a formal complaint. He was sentenced to death.

There was no appeal process and the sentence was carried out immediately. The five who had been banned were told they must stay west of the western boundaries of Louisiana, Arkansas, Missouri, Iowa and Minnesota. They must not attempt to communicate with anyone east of that line. Being caught and convicted of attempting to break the rules of the ban would result in an automatic lifetime ban and a death sentence for a second occurrence. The prisoners were given two days to collect what they wanted to take with them then put in a small bus and driven to Shreveport. They were told to start walking west and not to stop until they were in Texas. It was determined that the two men to be charged with the castration and garroting of two citizens were among the four killed by the first and only burst of fire by the army. The rest of the guardsmen were tried even though absent and sentenced to shunning for one year. The location of these men was known because they had been secretly trailed to the location in Columbus where they were holed up. Leaflets bearing the names of every one of them were dropped. The leaflets explained their punishment and stressed that their sentences didn't commence until they had returned and surrendered. The pilots of the small planes delivering the leaflets returned and reported that they had seen men picking up and reading them so there was no question that the message had been delivered.

Another problem was resolved at the same time by a joint statement by the President, Supreme Court and Congress. The statement simply said that any woman who had been forced or coerced into a marriage not of her choosing could have the marriage annulled by appearing before a district judge with three witnesses to the event. The men involved were forbidden from any interference in the process with the threat of banning if they did so. A total of twenty-six women took advantage of the ruling and all were declared to be unmarried with their maiden names restored. There was only one overt act of resistance to the ruling. A fifty-two year old man who publicly stated, "No ruling by an amateur politician or shyster lawyer was going to prevent him from asserting his rights as a married man." He was shot and killed by the brother of the woman involved while trying to force his way into the home where the woman had sought shelter. The guardsmen who had fled from Tuscaloosa began to trickle back two or three at a time. They were escorted to court where their sentences were read and were then escorted to a house or apartment to begin serving their time. Two of the guards had sworn they were never returning to the restrictions of society. They had shouldered their packs and headed into the interior of Mississippi.

Later that winter Scout Team Six discovered human bones, two chewed up packs and two rusted rifles just east of Vicksburg. It was assumed but never verified that it was the remains of the two guardsmen.

The remainder of the Tuscaloosa refugees was soon assimilated into their chosen communities and the various church groups found there. The Tuscaloosa Experiment, as the event was commonly referred to, was considered closed.

Chapter 21 ----- 2131

With the Tuscaloosa issue settled Chris and Pete returned to planning the retrieval of Pete's plane from Perry. Pete suggested that they include Brendon in their plan with the idea of restoring the VTOL plane which had been so useful in Iowa. Rascal and Jib had agreed to go along. More importantly both of their wives had given their blessing to the endeavor. The VTOL had a limited range but by using the fuel stops set up on US-65 they could fly it from Perry to Montgomery. Carol expressed a wish to go along on the flight. She had discussed it with Phoebe who assured her there was plenty of room for Chris and Carol's four teenagers to stay at the Hintz home for as long as Carol would be gone.

Two additional passengers were added to the manifest for the flight. Dr. Megan Conrad, the Secretary of Education was going along to check on the status of the schools set up for the few children of the families which remained in Iowa. Diane Finnegan as Secretary of the Interior and Industry wanted to look at the general welfare of the people who had remained. There had been speculation whether the stay behinds had stayed widely scattered or had coalesced into a more tightly knit community.

Chris and Pete took off from Maxwell at seven a.m. on August 3, with six passengers and most of the tools belonging to Rascal and Jib. The flight took just under two hours. They made a low slow pass over the length of the runway and seeing no obstructions or obvious trash they landed then taxied to the hangar where the VTOL and Pete's plane had been stored. There were two men working on a small single engine plane in front of the next hangar on the line. The two men recognized the four dismounting from the plane and strolled over to greet them. After saying hello the men assured Rascal that he would find his planes in good shape except for a little dust. They said they had been sure that Pete and Brendon would return for their planes one day. They were at the airport on a daily basis and no one had been in the hangar except to check for frozen water lines during the winter which had been a very cold one. The newcomers were told that a shop two building up the line held a half dozen small electric cars and trucks connected to a charging grid and ready to drive.

The three women each selected a car and departed to Perry to look for sleeping quarters to use while they were in the area. Carol wanted to see the small medical clinic which had been set up prior to the move to Alabama. She told Chris she would return to pick him up by four that afternoon. It took the other two women less than three hours to have their questions answered. There was no organized school system. What little education taking place was occurring at home. Without leaving Perry, Diane discovered that as expected, the majority of the people had concentrated in one area. She assumed it was for company and mutual support. They had settled in a strip between Perry and Dawson and extending three to four miles south of highway 141.

At the airport both the VTOL and the twin jet appeared ready to fly. One of the four place small planes was in the hangar and it was decided to prepare it for flight as well. All of the fluids, including fuel, were drained from the planes and purged with air. In three days the planes were ready. All of the engines were turned over for some time without actually starting them. The planes were towed outside where the engines were started then taxi and brake tests were performed. When the men were satisfied that all systems were operating properly the three planes were subjected to several takeoffs and landings. The two men who had greeted the contingent from Alabama were both single and both of them were pilots. They had been working on their plane with the idea of flying it south. With very little persuasion they agreed to abandon their plane and fly the four- seater belonging to Chris and Brendon to Montgomery. The plane had enough range to make the flight with only one stop at Fort Knox for fuel.

Carol's visit to the clinic came at a very propitious time. The doctor who had stayed to manage the clinic was a patient there. He had been trampled by stampeding cattle being chased by a pack of wolves. He had suffered both a fractured arm and leg. When Carol arrived at the clinic she was greeted by the sight of the doctor encased in two casts. The nurse and medical technician were both on the verge of hysteria. There was only one other patient but it was a young woman who had been labor for thirty-six hours with no sign of an impending birth. Carol quickly scrubbed, donned surgical scrubs and examined the woman. She had the woman moved to the OR and performed the first C-section of her medical career. When the mother had recovered from the anesthetic she was presented with a twelve pound baby girl who seemed to be angry at the world and determined to display it. The cries were the loudest Carol had ever heard from a newborn and were quieted only when the child was put to her mother's breast. While the baby was nursing the mother and her husband asked Carol what her name was. They explained that they knew her as Dr. Weddle but they didn't know her given name. When she told them it was Carol Janine, the husband, named Patrick Michael Connery said he had a request. He told Carol that without her he would not have either his wife or daughter and he wanted to name the baby after her. Carol was pleased as well as flattered and gave her consent.

When his wife didn't arrive to pick him up by six that evening Chris went looking for her. He found her at the clinic holding a baby and looking pleased with herself. On seeing Chris, Carol blushed a deep red and started to apologize. She said she couldn't believe she had completely forgotten about him. Chris told her no apology was necessary as it was obvious what had kept her occupied.

When the planes were ready for the flight south Chris asked for a meeting of all the residents of the area. When they had assembled Chris asked them to reconsider moving to Alabama. He pointed out that while their crops looked promising there was no place to dispose of them and that they still had the harvest from the previous year in storage. Chris told them there were thousands of acres of good farm land in Georgia, Alabama and Mississippi and a surplus of jobs for those who chose not to continue farming. He stressed the importance of education and told them of the school system established in the south which included the college level of study. Chris finished his talk by pointing out the much superior medical help available in the south. Chris had barely finished his speech when a burly, gray haired man stood up. Without preamble he began speaking. "Two months ago my wife died from a burst appendix. Three days ago my daughter and granddaughter would have died if Dr. Weddle had not arrived. If for no reason other than the medical aspect, I am ready to go south. I and my family will be prepared to move in two weeks. I would like a show of hands from the others here who are ready to join me." To the surprise of the contingent from Alabama the vote was nearly unanimous. Chris rose to his feet again and waited for the crowd to become quiet. He told them it would require a month to get the food and fuel stops fully stocked. After that time there should be no problems for the travelers. He promised to have centers set up in both Birmingham and Montgomery to assist the newcomers choose where they wished to settle.

Chapter 22 ----- 2131

While the Montgomery group was preparing for the flight home Carol told Chris she wanted to put the new mother, Cheryl Connery, and the baby on the plane and take them home with them. It would only be for six weeks or so until Michael arrived and she wanted to be sure Cheryl had the proper care until she was well enough to care for herself and the baby. She would give Craig's room to the mother and baby and Craig could move in with Chris Jr. for a short time. Chris commented that once Kathie got her hands on the baby, the rest of them would not have much to do about caring for the new Carol Janine. Two seats were folded down in the Weddle jet to provide Cheryl a comfortable ride. Both Jib and Rascal took a turn at holding the baby. "For practice," the both said. All four flights were uneventful. Brendon spent a night parked beside a fuel station and arrived before noon of the second day.

When they arrived home the Weddles were greeted by three teenagers and a four year old who were elated to have their parents home. The teenagers were just happy to be back in their own rooms and daily routine. Four year old Linda Ann clung to her mother and Carol, for the first few days, spent most of every day with Linda clinging to her knee or cuddled in the crook of her arm.

When Brendon came home two days after the others he noticed that Phoebe and the two girls seemed excited about something. When he asked about it they told him he was letting his imagination run away and that he was just spoiled and homesick after only six days away from the family.

In late afternoon Brendon Jr. and his wife Donna drove in. Phoebe told Brendon she had invited them for supper that evening. After the customary hugs Phoebe said Jr. had something to tell his father. Brendon, expecting an announcement that Donna was pregnant smiled and said he was looking forward to becoming a grandfather. Jr. smiled back and said, "That too Dad, we were going to tell everyone at supper but this is something else. I found something and couldn't find anywhere else to get it out of the weather, so I put it in your barn. I would like you to look at it and see if you think it is something we can use or if I should just return it to where I found it." At this point Phoebe told them to go look at it now. She didn't need them cluttering up the house while she was preparing a family dinner and trying to get the table set. Brendon pointed out that she had Donna and her own daughters to help her. Phoebe didn't respond verbally, she just gave him the "look" and pointed to the back door. As they were walking to the barn Jr. commented that his mother was a bit snappish today. Brendon smiled and said, "Son that was just for show. When you turned toward the door she winked at me and that is always a sign she is pleased." When they entered the barn Brendon was instantly aware of nickering and stamping hooves that seemed too deep and heavy to have come from Spot. In the last two box stalls stood two giant horses. They were Clydesdales and they looked identical except one had three white feet and stocking and the other had four. Brendon asked where they had come from and why they were here. Jr. replied they had belonged to an elderly gentleman, who lived just outside of Prattville, who could no longer care for them. He added that Brendon had done so much for the family and community that he deserved to be rewarded. Brendon asked for the names of the horses and was told they didn't yet have names. He had been calling them Three and Four because of their feet colors but naming them was up to Brendon. Brendon told his son the names were appropriate and would stand as Jr. had called the horses. Jr. then explained the horses were only two years old and would grow to be even larger than they now were. The mares which had foaled them were full sisters and had been bred to the same stallion. They had been raised more as pets than as draft animals so tending them was like caring for a pair of two thousand pound puppies. Brendon turned the horses out into the pasture next to the barn then stood and watched as they bucked, ran and gamboled like the youngsters they were. After a few minutes the horses, having worked off their exuberance, returned to the men for a scratching and neck rubbing session. The horses were given a feed of oats and left with the barn door open so they could return to the pasture. Jr. remarked that both cougars and possibly a grizzly bear had been seen in the area so he had been locking the horses in the barn at night.

When the men returned to the house Phoebe hugged Brendon while she turned to Jr. and said, "He left the names as Three and Four didn't he?" Jr. nodded yes and Phoebe said, "I know this man, he is always thinking of the other person. Three, Four and Spot, what a set of names for a horse herd."

Carol had moved Cheryl and the baby into Craig's room and Kathie, as predicted had quickly taken over every aspect of Carol Janine's care except feeding her which by necessity fell to Cheryl. Linda Ann was captivated by the baby and insisted on holding her from time to time.

Diane Finnigan got the fuel and supply trucks rolling and in three weeks the rest stops were ready for the migration from Iowa. Pete made a number of flights to Perry taking some medications plus maps to show the travelers where the fuel stations were located. Pete was given a list of the people making the trek. It turned out that every person known to be living in Iowa with one exception was on the list. The lone holdout was a man living in a house above the river just outside of Minburn. The man who was fifty-four years old had a sixteen year old son who was mentally limited and did not cope well in any social setting. The man, named Charlie Engels, felt the boy would have a better life if he lived where he didn't need to deal with other people. When this information reached Health Secretary Helen Smith and Education Secretary, Megan Conrad they were both embarrassed that this boy had escaped their attention. The two women asked and were given permission for Pete to fly them to Perry. They found a car and driver and were taken to the home of Charlie and Duane. Over a two day period they found Duane could read at a beginning first grade level and could print his name. The women convinced father and son they could, in five years, have the boy capable of reading and writing at a level which would enable him to hold a job and support himself. This information quelled Charlie's greatest fear which was what would happen to Duane when he became too old to care for him. When the women were ready for their flight home Charlie and Duane had packed their belongings in a small truck and were in Perry waiting to join a convoy heading south.

Chapter 23 ----- 2131

As the summer passed scanty reports started to come in from the six scout groups of the Discovery Corps and the ship Discovery. Team One had found a group of survivors in Lake City, Florida. There were seventeen people in the group, four of who were too old or feeble to travel unless by vehicle. Twelve of the group had the telltale marks on their hips while the remainder showed no clue to why they had survived. A convoy of six electric vehicles was assembled. The convoy included a small truck carrying a generator to charge the batteries in case highway charging stations could not be found when needed. Brad Sweet went with the group in the event that immediate medical help was required. Medical care for the Florida group had, for twenty-four years, been in the hands of a man who was a young EMT with the Gainesville fire department on the day the world ended.

Team One stressed that they were all well. They requested permission to spend the winter in or near Savannah so they could make their search of South Carolina and southern Georgia without needing to rush. Their request was granted and they were told to report the location of their winter quarters once established.

Team Two reported no signs of humans until they were in the extreme north east corner of Georgia. There in an area of several square miles which contained Sugar Maple trees they found many of the trees had been tapped to collect sap. They also found a small shed containing a cooker for boiling the sap down to make syrup. The bulk of North Carolina appeared empty with no sign of people to be found. When they reached western North Carolina and eastern Tennessee they were amazed to find a thriving community of eighteen to twenty thousand people. They were primarily of Native American descent with a scattering of whites. The largest groups were of Cherokee and Choctaw heritage with a smattering of other tribal roots. Many of them had migrated from Oklahoma immediately after the "Bad Day" as they referred to it. For the most part they lived in cabins and houses and planted extensive gardens. They also maintained substantial herds of cattle and swine plus poultry. They were not interested in moving to join the Alabama population but expressed a desire to open a line of communication with them. They were especially eager to obtain some of the technology being used in Alabama. The wind turbines of the Cheyenne were of great interest as they had been without electricity from the very beginning. The group agreed to send a delegation to Montgomery immediately to commence a dialogue between the groups.

Scout Team Three found no one in Virginia until they reached the coast. Here they located a few scattered individuals who were subsisting primarily on seafood and small vegetable gardens. They occasionally had venison or the stray beef but seafood was easier to obtain so they didn't put much effort into hunting. These people had been isolated for so long that they spoke very little. To a person they stressed that they had no interest in rejoining society and they only wished to live out their lives in seclusion. The only exception to this was a pair of twins. They were a girl and boy fifteen or sixteen years of age. They had always been called simply girl or boy. They had left the hut where they lived with an older woman and followed the troop for over a week before being discovered. They begged to be allowed to travel with the troop until people were found who would take them in. The scouts discussed the situation and decided to take the two with them to Alabama. The two were given the names George and Martha after it was explained to them that boy and girl were only words to explain they were male and female. Neither of the two could read or write and their vocabulary was very limited. One of the women scouts took the illiteracy as a challenge and began searching stores for primary reading books and writing materials. By the time they arrived back in Montgomery she would have both of the young people reading at a second grade level and writing or printing the alphabet and simple words. They found no other survivors and arrived home in mid-October.

Team Four and Team Five found not a single person in the east and north, only desolation and complete emptiness. Both teams were forced to shoot a number of aggressive bears, both Black and Grizzly, which refused to let them pass.

Team Five shot a male African lion which charged them outside of Madison, Wisconsin. All of the teams reported seeing exotic animals. Exotic meaning, species not native to North America. Escapees no doubt from zoos and animal preserves.

Team Six which was traveling along the Gulf Coast found survivors all along their route. There were groups ranging in size from fifty to five hundred persons. They were surviving on food from the Gulf and from home gardens. Most of these people were from the north and mid-west. They had migrated individually and in small groups to escape the bitter winters in the north. They had coalesced into larger groups for company and mutual support. The team had turned north at Galveston and traveled as far as Dallas before turning east to return home. They estimated that they had been in contact with five to seven thousand people. About half of that number expressed interest in moving to Alabama and joining the community there. The primary reason for wanting to move was the availability of better medical care. In the end about twenty-three hundred people took to the road for the trek to Alabama.

By the end of 2131 the known population in the area which had been the USA had almost doubled. Of course, not all of them were citizens of the New United States. It was generally thought that eventually they would all join to form one political entity.

By October the required amount of money had been coined and printed and the distribution to the citizens began. As expected there were a few people who attempted to collect their allotment at more than one location. When apprehended these individuals were shunned for sixty days and their allotment was cut by half. The banks were soon virtually bulging with money and the few printing plants were printing checks in great numbers. There were a few robberies and when caught the robbers were banned for two years. Two people, a man and a woman, were executed for having shot their victims during the course of the robbery.

In October, Congress passed an act awarding each adult coming into the US the same amount given to each established citizen. The newcomers were required to declare their citizenship and take an oath of allegiance to the New United States.

After the Discovery had sailed in March radio communication had been spotty and by the middle of April had ceased completely. The ship had cruised the Gulf Coast of Texas and by the time it reached Tampico on the Mexican coast there were no longer any messages arriving in Mobile. It had been agreed before the ship sailed that her mission was to continue even if the communication system failed.

In Mobile a small, one hundred sixty-five foot, Navy gunship was towed to a dry dock and feverish activity was begun to restore her to duty status. While this was happening, one hundred men were recruited, sworn into a newly created U.S. Navy and began training to take the ship to sea. The ship was renamed the USS Halsey in honor of a fighting Admiral from almost two hundred years in the past. In a somewhat "tongue in cheek" gesture she was given the number NBB-1, BB being the designation for battleship of the Admiral Halsey era with the N indicating new.

Chapter 24 ----- 2131

When Scout Team Three arrived home with the two young people Phoebe immediately took charge. She announced that George and Martha needed a home and family and she could provide both. Junior's room was empty and Letha's room was large enough for Martha to move in with her. There were boxes of clothing and shoes in the attic. Phoebe added that her kids plus Chris and Carol's three oldest could be effective tutors with the newcomers school work.

There were many adjustments for everyone but the household gradually settled into a routine. Both Martha and George were apt pupils and both pursued their education as if starved for the written word. George was quick to pick up mathematics and seemed destined to find a career in some branch of engineering. Martha was drawn to medicine and decided early that she wanted to pursue education in either nursing or as an MD. With Brendon Jr. taking on the responsibility of the farming for the families, George was soon in full charge of the community livestock. He did the milking and feeding but his greatest joy came from caring for the two Clydesdales. In two months he had made pets of them. Within four months, with Brendon's help, he had fitted harness to them and drove them around the property albeit without a wagon or farm implements behind them. At the suggestion of Chris and with his assistance, the parade harness once worn by the Belgians was adjusted to fit Three and Four. At first the horses resisted the idea of wearing bells but with a lot of petting and stroking from George they came to accept the noise. In fact, it seemed they stepped a little higher and moved more briskly when wearing the bells.

In Mobile, in a compound which had been the winter quarters of a small traveling circus, Chris found the wagon for which he had been searching. It was high wheeled with hard rubber tires. It had a large box which would seat eighteen to twenty and was gaudily painted. Chris had the paint touched up and the axles greased.

While Brendon was on a week's long trip to the settlement in east Tennessee Chris had the wagon trucked to Montgomery. George hitched the team to the wagon and they responded as if they had been pulling a wagon for years. When Brendon returned home he was greeted by a small parade. George had the team and wagon groomed and polished to perfection. All of the neighborhood youngsters plus Carol, Melinda and Jackie were riding in the wagon. Having been coached by Phoebe, George doffed his cap and with a sweeping bow, handed the reins to Brendon while stating, "Here is your team Squire Hintz." From the moment Brendon mounted the drivers' seat and clicked the team into motion it was obvious something was wrong. The horses fought the bit, shuffled their feet with their heads down. They seemed unsure of what was expected of them. Brendon drove them up the street and took a turn through the Fox Run area. He returned to the Wolf Song neighborhood and asked George to join him on the driver's seat. He handed the reins to the boy and asked him to drive up the street. There was an instant change in the horses. Their heads came up and their steps became high and crisp. After only a block or so George was asked to turn the team around and return home. Whey they had stopped and the onlookers had gathered around Brendon spoke to the group. He said, "It appears this young man has lied to me." There was an audible gasp from the group and a look of puzzlement on the face of George. With a broad smile Brendon resumed speaking, "This young man presented me with the reins and told me here was my team. After driving some distance and then watching him do the same it is obvious that this is not my team. There is a bond between George and these animals that should not be tampered with. The horses and all of the gear belong to George and my only wish is that they have a long and happy association." He added that he now had a sense of what Chris felt when his dogs deserted him for Melinda and Carol.

Chapter 25 ----- 2132

At the January Wolf Song supper Chris announced that the Discovery was due in Mobile in two weeks. The ship reported it had major news but wanted to wait until they were home to report. The news was such that it was going to change the lives of everyone. The meteorologists had also said they had a major release of information about ready to present and it would also be a potential life changer for much of the population.

Mavis told the group she was pregnant again that Grandma Wilson was going to have another set of twins to spoil.

Brendon and Chris made a joint announcement. Neither man was going to seek nor accept a term in any government office. Both of them had devoted the better part of fifteen years to the community. Now they were going into business together and with any luck it would occupy them for the rest of their working lives. Their idea was to form a seed company which would supply seed and plants for everything from garden flowers to farm crops. Brendon was turning his machinery restoration business over to the four men he had first hired. Chris then announced that he had given up on the idea of returning to a place in the composite plant. Lance was a capable manager and with his one-fourth interest in the concern could be trusted to keep it growing. The company was beginning to turn a healthy profit and was going to provide more income than his family would need to be comfortable. He was, therefore, going to divide his three-fourths share equally between himself and his cousins Brendon and Jackie. Between the three of them they would still control any major actions of the company.

As they lingered at the table to wait for the wolf chorus to begin, Martha commented that it was a lovely way to spend an evening. She said, "To be surrounded by good friends, in shirt sleeve weather with the scent of early flowers in the air, it just couldn't be much better. Down to earth Phoebe spoke next. She said, "Martha is absolutely correct, but I have been sitting her thinking how much I miss sitting on the deck in Iowa in winter, bundled up for the cold and listening to the Raccoon River wolves sing for us." It was quiet for a moment, than Carol patted Phoebe's hand and said, "I miss them too."

A group of citizens had formed a committee and decided they wanted to have a parade on April 7. The date was being referred to as New World Day and the committee wanted to have it recognized as an official holiday. George reported he had been asked to lead the parade with his team and circus wagon. Jack Wilson had been selected to preside as Grand Marshal and have a prominent seat in the circus wagon. After George had made his announcement the Wolf Song gathering began to break up. Tomorrow was a working day and there were still some little ones who were up beyond their usual bed time.

Chapter 26 ----- 2132

Chris and Brendon both attended the meeting held to hear the report of the weather and climate experts. There was a committee of nine people from the Congress, three Senators and six Representatives. What the eleven observers heard was, to say the least, both mind-boggling and jaw-dropping in scope. The current winter reports from the north indicated a much milder winter than the past few years. Star sightings and computer modeling indicated the earth was returning to the axis it had been on prior to the "day." Satellite photos were showing that the ice cap in the north had shown little growth in the past year and in two areas had actually receded by a very small amount. The "experts," while conceding that they were really only guessing, predicted that within five years the climate would return to the status it had been in prior to the "day." Chris and Brendon called for an emergency meeting of the Wolf Song and Fox Run communities that evening.

After relating what they had heard in the report that day the two men waited for comments. In unison and sounding as if they had rehearsed it Phoebe and Jackie asked, "Does this mean we can go home?" Carol added, "Yes, I want to return home and the sooner the better." The men were surprised by the ardor and pleading in the voices of the women. They had surmised that the women had been uprooted and moved enough in their lifetimes that they would have no wish to move again. Chris understood them. His heart and mind were still bound to the house and land which had been his home and refuge since he was eighteen years old. Chris pointed out that he still had a year to serve as President. Phoebe was quick to counter that he had an airplane and it was only a two and a half hour flight from Montgomery to Perry. He could fill his presidential obligations in three days in Montgomery and spend the rest of the week at home. A clamorous voice vote was taken and was very nearly unanimous. The people from Fox Run were invited to join the move and with the exception of Dyan they all voted to go north. Dyan told them she had the first real home of her adult life and had no intention of leaving it until she was carried out in a box.

Most of the vehicles they had used in the move south were still in the possession of the group and could be used again. The women were arguing for an early departure date but were persuaded to wait until April 9 so George and Jack could participate in the New World Day parade.

The next day Chris had a meeting with John McCleary. John was asked whether if Chris resigned the office of President he, John, would serve out the remainder of the term. John replied yes, but only for this term as it was his intention to return to Iowa also. The two men were not sure of the procedure so they drafted a statement and sent copies to both Congress and the Supreme Court. March tenth was designated as the date for the transfer of office to occur.

Once again the hectic sorting of what to take and what to leave began. This time the choices were easier to make and the mood of the community was, for the most part, much lighter than it had been the first time.

While the packing and sorting activity was occurring the Discovery returned to Mobile. The news the Discovery crew brought was at least as momentous as that of the weather experts had been. The biggest item was that a strip of land spanning the South American continent had been totally unaffected by the virus of 2106. The "virus free" zone stretched approximately from the 20 degree to the 30 degree south parallels of latitude, a span of about seven hundred miles. Outside of their immediate borders the people of the zone had done no exploring. With the total failure of all international communications they assumed the rest of the world was dead. They had spent the past twenty-five years trying to rebuild their economies. The fragments of the surviving countries had retained their political identities. They had been discussing the possibility of forming one county on the pattern of the old United States. Each existing country would become a state within the larger entity. The talks were moving slowly as it was extremely difficult of a people to give up their national identity. There was an instant question of whether the virus free strip extended across the Atlantic and southern Africa. The only way to make that determination was to send the two ships to the west coast of the "Dark Continent" and possibly around the Cape and up the east coast as well. To a man, the crews of the both ships volunteered to make the voyage as soon as the ships could be prepared for sea again. The last bit of news which had been purposely saved as a surprise was that the Discovery had a ton and half of green coffee beans in her hold plus two dozen crates of green bananas. The committee was told that the warehouses in Brazil, Chile and Argentina were bulging with coffee, fruit and other products such as cotton and wool cloth. The people in South American were anxious to trade for technology and especially medical products. There were scattered pockets of survivors all along the coast of Mexico, Central and South America. Most of them were of Indian blood with a few white and black individuals in the mix. The majority of these survivors were from miles inland. They seemed to have gravitated to the coastal areas in hope of finding a more plentiful food supply. Many of them still thought of North America as the land of milk and honey and begged to be taken aboard the ship for transport to the US, unaware that it no longer existed as they had known it. With limited resources due to the small population, the rehabilitation of cargo ships was going to be a slow process. It was estimated that no more than one ship per year could be made seaworthy.

Chapter 27 ----- 2133

While the population was buzzing with speculation about the possible changes the news from the Discovery would bring, the Wolf Song and Fox Run groups continued their preparations for moving north. Christ received a visit from Jonathon. Jonathon told him if there were no major objections the Cheyenne people wanted to return to their homes in Carroll County. While Carroll County was not the Great Plains which had been their home for centuries, it was a rich and nurturing area which they had come to love. Chris replied that he and his group would be happy to have their old neighbors in place again. It would also eliminate the problem of how Phoebe was going to react to being separated from her daughter and grandchildren.

In March the transfer of office from Chris to John took place with little fanfare.

On April 7 the parade was held. It was led by George driving his team with Jack Wilson seated in a throne like chair with most of the women and children from Wolf Song in the wagon with him. Most of the parade was made up of children and young people leading or riding their pets. There were goats, cattle, horses and even two chickens on leashes. Several clowns frolicked about as they handed out pieced of homemade molasses candy. A five piece marching band provided music. They were often out of tune with each other but no one seemed to care or notice. The tail end of the parade consisted of twenty Cheyenne men mounted on spotted horses and dressed as if for a Buffalo hunt two hundred fifty years in the past.

The parade route was less than a half mile long and halfway through tragedy struck. Jack slumped over in his chair and despite having two skilled doctors in the wagon could not be revived. Martha was in the wagon and she insisted they finish the parade. When they read Jack's will that night they discovered a very simple document. Jack left everything he owned to Martha. He asked that there be no funeral, that he be cremated and that his ashes, if possible, be buried beside his brother in Iowa. At a later date he would like to have Martha's ashes placed beside his own.

The statement added that Martha and Charlie had been the two most important people in his life and he wanted to spend eternity with both of them by his side. The next day the cremation took place and the ashes delivered to Martha in a brass urn. Brendon offered to find a secure place in the furniture van for the urn. Martha told them if no one minded she would like to carry the urn with her during the ride to Iowa. She added that it would give her some comfort to have Jack close by during the long drive.

Chapter 28 ----- 2133

On April 9 at just after sunrise the caravan pulled out and got on route 65 headed north. They had debated about taking a different route but decided that since it was somewhat familiar it would be simpler to just return by the road they had driven on the trip south. The two women who had been rescued in Tennessee asked that they please not stop at the rest area where their rescue had taken place the location evoked too many bad memories. Carol and Melinda were also happy to just pass the place where they had each killed a man. In the same circumstances both women would do the same thing again but it was not an event they wished to dwell upon.

Except for detouring and finding new routes to get around three fallen bridges, the trip was uneventful. The adults were much impressed from the first day by the solicitude shown to Martha, Doreen, who was married to Hans and to Sven who was the oldest of the group. Whenever one of the elders got out of a vehicle on creaky knees there was one of the teenagers standing by with a helping hand to an elbow. The young ones were quick with an offer to refresh a drink or fetch another piece of chicken form the communal pot. It became almost a badge of honor to be allowed to carry Jack's urn while supporting Martha's elbow with the other hand.

On the third day of the journey Carol took Chris Jr. aside and asked him about the sudden concern of the young for the old in the group. The boy, with tears welling in his eyes told his mother he felt terrible. No one in their family had ever died before and he had never even considered the possibility. He had never told Grandpa Jack that he loved him or said thank you for all of the things Grandpa had done for the family. Jr. had called all of the

123

young people together and they had discussed the situation. The others had felt essentially the same as Jr. and they had made a pact. No person and in particular the elderly in the community was going to be un-thanked for their deeds or untold that they were loved. When they needed a helping hand there would be one or more ready to help. Carol hugged her son, kissed his cheek and repeated what she had said to his father many times. "You are a good man Mr. Weddle."

The caravan arrived in the Wolf Song area in late morning of their fifth day on the road. They unloaded only the livestock and their personal items then everyone pitched in to dust, mop and wash dishes. All of the electrical systems were still working and after cleaning it Chris turned on the big outside grill. He took a ham plus a rack of smoked pork chops out of the freezer truck, put them on the grill and soon the aroma of their first meal at home was wafting about the property.

Hans and Doreen were anxious to move on to her old home southeast of Carroll. They were persuaded to spend the night and get a fresh start the next day. Melinda intended to send the twins, Aaron and Janis with them to help clean and insure the house was habitable. Sven and Rachael were also in a hurry to get home but were also persuaded to wait for the new day. Mary Lou, Gordon and the two girls would go with them and stay until they were settled then Gordon wanted to find a small farm close by. Sven was becoming somewhat frail and both Gordon and Mary Lou felt they would be needed to help rehabilitate Sven's orchard. The women had pulled canned, frozen and fresh fruit and vegetables out of the food truck. At seven that evening they sat down to a feast. Chris had never imagined this much humanity gathering at his home. There were forty-five people present and many were eating from baking dishes and pie tins. Jib was even using a small fry pan for a plate. When they had finished eating and were idly chatting Phoebe stood and looked at the group until all the talking ceased. As Phoebe began to speak it was easy for all to see the tears in her eyes and detect the catch in her voice. She said, "I have a proposition to make for all of you to vote on. You newcomers may not be aware that for years we have held monthly Wolf Song suppers. My proposal is that from today the April supper be called the Coming Home Supper and that it be held on the anniversary of this date, April 13, and that we hold it in the shelter house so we have enough parking and seating for all." The group instantly approved without a show of hands. They shouted, whistled and stamped their feet in approval. Chris stood up and when the group quieted he said, "I think that can be taken as a yes vote, thank you Phoebe." At this point Chris and Carol's daughter Linda Ann, who at age 5 was the baby of the Wolf Song community, was standing in her seat waving her arms. For the most part she was being ignored. Chris Jr. moved some plates then lifted his little sister and stood her on the table at the same time he loosed a loud piercing whistle. There was instant silence and Linda Ann in a quiet voice asked if she could speak. Hans in his most courtly voice replied, "My dear you speak as long as you like, if anyone interrupts I will hold them in contempt of court." Linda Ann began, she said, "I know everyone heard the woofies in our other home but it wasn't the same as our woofies here at our real home. Here they are louder. When I was little," this brought a chuckle from the group, "it scared me. One night I was sitting in Aunt Melinda's lap hiding my face. I peeked out and saw my mommy and daddy holding hands and smiling and I knew it was alright. Now I can't wait to hear them again. So don't be afraid, they love us." She then added, "Uncle Hans, now that Grandpa Jack is gone, may I call you Grandpa Hans? I really need a Grandpa and mommy said I had to ask you. One more thing, what is contempt of court?" Hans found it difficult to answer due to a sudden limp in his throat so he smiled and nodded yes. Jr. lifted Linda Ann back to the floor. She walked directly to Hans who lifted her into his lap. In a matter of minutes she was asleep. It had been a long, tiring day for a little girl. As if on cue the wolf chorus began. The little girl stirred and mumbled, "Don't be afraid."

After the dishes, pots and pans were washed and put away the group began to scatter to find their beds. Everyone was accommodated in one of the Wolf Song homes. The adults in beds with the youngsters on the floor in their traveling bed rolls or sleeping bags. With the wolf song still echoing in the night Carol told Chris that their daughter had made Hans a very happy old man that night.

Chapter 29 ----- 2133

The morning of April 14 was hectic. It had been decided the previous evening that breakfast for all was to be oatmeal, fresh milk and frozen applesauce. Chris was bemoaning the fact that he had no way to roast any of the twenty pounds of coffee beans he had brought out of Alabama. Doreen who with Hans had spent the night with the Weddles said, "For goodness sakes Chris, get me the beans and I will show you how we did it on the Reservation in Dakota." She took a large flat bottomed skillet out of a cabinet dumped in a half pound of coffee beans she weighed on the kitchen scale. With the heat on medium and stirring constantly she asked Chris if he wanted dark or light coffee. Chris and Hans both answered dark and the same time. In due time, Doreen pronounced the beans ready. Chris put them through the grinder, loaded the coffee maker and in minutes the kitchen was filled with, to Chris at least, the wonderful aroma of fresh coffee. Doreen, Hans and Chris filled mugs and took them out to the deck to enjoy the morning. When they were seated Chris looked across the table and after taking his first sip of coffee said, "I love you Doreen Wilhelm." Doreen winked at him, smiled and said, "You need to be careful with the sweet talk mister or Hans will be challenging you to a duel." While they were finishing their coffee the wireless phones began to beep at them. It was Molly and Patty announcing to all of them that both women, although 45 years of age, were pregnant. Reggie and Richard were both stunned but extremely pleased. Both women thought they were due in early November. Melinda who was going to set up a temporary clinic in one of the houses at the school complex insisted they come to see her as soon as everyone was settled.

Hans and Doreen with the twins who were going to help them move in prepared to leave for Carroll. The teachers, Frank and Nadine were going to look at the house where they had previously lived in the school complex. Reggie, Richard and their now pregnant wives were going to look in the ruins of Dawson. They thought they could find enough usable material to build at least three houses on existing foundations. They were going to be joined in their endeavor by Peggy and her husband Steve White plus her daughters Nadine and Marilyn. Martha had been invited and had accepted the invitation to live with Pete and Jackie. She was promised that if she changed her mind the group would build her a small house close to one of the older places. Brendon Jr. had his eye on a place a short half mile west of where his parents lived. The house had been empty for twenty-five years and no one knew the condition of the interior. It did have a decent looking set of brick tile out-buildings which counted as a major plus with Brendon Jr.

The area became a beehive of activity. The women soon had the houses in order and moved outside to work with the men to clear the yards of weeds, brush and the countless saplings which had sprung up in their five year absence. They pulled out the smaller ones and dug up those they couldn't pull. Chris took his large tractor and tilled all five gardens plus plots at the school compound for the two couples there. Brendon Sr. and Jr. were working sixteen and eighteen hour days to prepare the farm ground for planting. Martha, of course, claimed the right to care for the little ones while the parents put in the long hours of labor. Sven and his extended family had moved into the orchard property south of Perry. There were two solid houses on the property which required extensive cleaning and some minor repairs. Mary Lou and Gordon decided rather than try to farm this year, they would stay at the orchard and assist Sven in getting it back in order. Sven said it was not too late to prune the trees and decide which ones needed to be replaced. He gave Gordon and Mary Lou a crash course in how and where to cut. Sven let them work the last two trees on their own. After examining the results he pronounced them ready to work the orchard when it was time to do so.

By the end of the first week of May all the gardens were planted. The two Brendons were working from dawn to dusk planting corn and soy beans. They decided that they had enough hay and oats in storage so they made no effort to renew those crops this year.

On May 3 they were surprised to see Jonathon and Mavis pull into the Hintz parking area. The couple reported that about two hundred of the Cheyenne were in a convoy on highway 141 heading for Carroll County. The rest of the tribe was also on the road, primarily on foot or using horse power. The twins who had gone to assist Hans and Doreen returned with the news that they were getting settled in Carroll. Doreen's little house on the river had burned to the ground so they had moved into the back part of the building Hans had used for an office in town. Mavis had miscarried her previous pregnancy some months before but reported she was pregnant again and expected to deliver twins around the middle of August. Phoebe immediately began suggesting that the young couple settle closer to home but Jonathon pointed out that unless he resigned his position as Chief of the Cheyenne he was obligated to live with his people.

After the hectic pace of cleaning, repairing and planting was over Martha announced it was time to place Jack's ashes beside his brother's body. Digging the grave was simple. Brendon extended the handle of a post hole auger and bored a hole six feet deep. When the hole was filled Martha planted a red rose bush in the top and told the group when her time came she would like a pink rose planted on her grave.

All summer a slow trickle of people came in from the south. For the most part they returned to the homes they had left five years before.

In August Mavis gave birth, not to twins as expected, but to triplets, two of whom were identical. She named them Jonathon, Brendon and Christopher. At the August Wolf Song supper Dyan and her husband Patrick appeared along with a two month old daughter. It was a big surprise to all but Mary Lou who had received word of their coming. When asked about her home in Montgomery and her vow to never leave it Dyan told them it had been difficult to leave but she had decided family was more important than houses. Mary Lou and Peggy were as close as sisters to her and she wanted to grow old with them as neighbors. Reggie, Richard and Steve had just finished their homes in Dawson and were moving in as they could find usable furniture. Richard had painted four signs and erected them on the four roads leading into town. The signs all read, "Village of New Home, Population 8 and growing." The three men offered to construct a home for Dyan and her family and the offer was quickly accepted.

It had been a warm summer with adequate rain. The gardens, although planted late, flourished and they were all busy freezing, canning and even drying the produce. The people who arrived too late to plant gardens were going to have a lean winter with a meat heavy diet. The Wolf Song people would share their garden bounty but first they must feed themselves. Chris had started a variety of garden vegetables in his greenhouse although it would not be an adequate amount to feed everyone. Brendon vowed that within two years he was going to have a greenhouse of his own.

For the first time in years there was no snow in October. There were several hard frosts which finished off any remaining flowers and garden vegetables.

Brendon, Chris and Pete while discussing their childhoods one day recalled the tradition of Jack-O-Lanterns. They each took two large pumpkins and carved faces into them. Putting a small, flickering lamp in each one they placed them by their front doors. The young people were intrigued and a flurry of pumpkin carving ensued.

Brendon Jr. and his wife Donna were living in one of the houses built for Sr's farm workers prior to the move south. The farmhouse the young couple had chosen needed extensive repairs and Jr. spent every hour he could spare from farming duties working on it. Donna was expecting in March and they wanted to move in before the baby arrived.

Molly and Patty both delivered their babies in November. Molly had a little girl, Carolyn, and Patty birthed a son, Robert.

Reggie and Richard were both ecstatic over the babies and couldn't get enough of holding them.

Brendon and Chris found four adjacent sections of land south of Dawson which were unclaimed. They posted signs claiming the land and began planning what they were going to plant in each section. They planned to devote one full section to growing nursery stock with every type of fruit and nut tree which would grow in Iowa. They realized it would be years before the concern became profitable. They felt that eventually the population would increase enough to support their venture.

In late November the balmy weather disappeared. Winter came in as if determined to make up for lost time. One snow storm followed another and road travel was next to impossible. Chris used his snow track machine between the homes in the Wolf Song community as well as the three families in Dawson. Most of them were now referring to Dawson as New Home as Richard had renamed the town on his signs.

Chapter 30 ----- 2134

The weather in January proved to be a continuation of that of December. There were frequent snows, bitter cold and unrelenting wind. Snow drifts piled up on the roads until travel was impossible. Chris Jr. and Craig snow shoed to the other homes. Between them they visited every house every day. Besides checking on the welfare of everyone the boys delivered fresh milk and eggs plus smoked meat from the smokehouses of Chris and Brendon. Craig always insisted on calling on the Sweets. He claimed it was because he enjoyed the extra exercise and fresh air. The adults were beginning to suspect there was a budding romance between Craig and Janis Marie.

Sven and his family, south of Perry, maintained contact through the radio phones and reported all was well with them. They had, by working long hours, managed to prune the entire orchard and had even removed a dozen old diseased trees.

January finally dragged to a close with one last storm which was the worst one of the winter. February produced a complete reversal of the weather. It warmed up and by the middle of the month the snow was gone except in shaded, sheltered places. In the northwest section of their selected four was a set of farm buildings which were still in good enough shape to be rehabilitated. The place was set up with a solar grid they were able to put back into operation. A large metal machine shop contained a charging grid and two electric tractors similar to what Chris had at home. There was enough other equipment that the men felt ready to start when the weather allowed. They had both planted a variety of fruit and nut seeds in their greenhouses and some of the tiny seedlings were already showing green tips.

In the first week of March word was received via radio that the ships Discovery and Admiral Halsey were planning to sail into Mobile around the first of April with more momentous news. Due to his past office and his influence in the community Chris was asked to be present for the briefing when the ships arrived. Chris asked Brendon to go with him then informed Reggie and Richard that if they had time for the job he would need his plane prepared for flight by April 1. Reggie called back to inform Chris the plane would be ready by March 20. Reggie added that he and Richard had discussed the situation and they had been Rascal and Jib to Chris for so many years they would prefer he use those names for them, especially when they were working on or around the airplane.

Chapter 31 ----- 2134

It was April 2, Chris and Brendon were in the air on their way to Mobile. They had taken time from their hectic schedule to attend this meeting and their plan was to return home on the 4th. The ships were due in Mobile today and the meeting would be held tomorrow. Since neither of them had any official standing they planned to attend the reading of the report then fly home. They were met at the airport by Jack Myers and shown to a room near both the cafeteria and the small auditorium for the meeting in the morning. They lingered in the cafeteria after their supper and chatted with individuals they had met on previous trips and during the five years they had lived in Alabama. There were also crew members from both ships but they were unable to glean any information about what they were going to hear the next morning.

Brendon and Chris were in bed early that night and up early the next morning. They had finished breakfast by 6:30 am and were seated in the auditorium well before the announced start time of 7:00 am. The room quickly filled and promptly at 7:00 John McCleary walked to the podium. He announced that it was a closed meeting and only those people on his list would be allowed to stay. As he called the roll there were two newspaper reporters and a number of interested citizens who were asked to leave. There would be a printed release available when the meeting was over. The reporters protested at their exclusion but were escorted out of the building after which the doors were locked and guards posted. The first report was by the group which had been designated to determine whether the virus free zone which extended across South America had continued across the Atlantic and then Africa. They zone had done exactly that. It had, in fact, broadened as it moved to the east. By the time it reached the east coast of Africa the zone had widened to cover an area which reached from 17 degrees to 33 degrees latitude. There were two theories regarding the existence of the zone and neither could be proven at this point in time. The first theory was that a wind pattern had developed which blew across two continents plus an ocean and had blown the virus to the sides and prevented it from falling into the zone. Unlikely but possible. The second possibility was that the orbits of the death dealing body had been such that gravity had pulled the virus to earth before it could spread to the free zone. This second theory seemed to be the most likely but it was stressed that it was still pure speculation. There were no experts on the subject and thus no expert opinions. The virus free zone in Africa included major portion of the countries of Namibia, Botswana, Zimbabawe, Mozambique and South Africa. It also included much of the island of Madagascar. There were five people seated on the stage who were introduced as citizens of Zimbabawe and South Africa. The spokesperson for the group was a woman of perhaps fifty years. She introduced herself as Linda Smithfield and told them she was a practicing attorney. She had grown up in Salisbury, Zimbabawe and had been in Johannesburg working on her doctorate in law when the end came. All of her family had perished and she had remained in South Africa. Linda introduced her fellow panel members as a railroad executive, a farmer, a police captain and a highway construction engineer. She added that all of them were prepared to answer any questions pertaining to their particular or related fields of expertise. Prior to the question period she had a series of proposals for the U.S. government to consider. She told the audience that there were as many as one hundred thousand people who were prepared to immigrate to the U.S. as soon as transportation could be arranged. Over the next ten to fifteen years she estimated up to a half million people would be looking for new homes. She suggested Congress establish a residency requirement of ten years before full voting citizenship would be granted, that all children born on U.S. soil be full citizens and that all newcomers be required to swear to adhere to U.S. law. The newcomers would be forbidden from claiming any property currently claimed by U.S. citizens. The Africans were prepared to accept any other reasonable rules and restrictions Congress might choose to impose. When asked why so many people were preparing to relocate the five South Africans said the native Africans were beginning to coalesce into their original tribal units. Already there had been tribal conflicts and the non-native Africans felt it was only a matter of time until the conflicts involved them. They felt it was better to leave on peaceful terms than to become involved in a never ending race war. The South Africans added that they would be able to supply and man the ships needed to transport their people across the Atlantic. Chris and Brandon stayed for the questioning period but asked no questions and tried to not draw any attention to themselves.

No one had a noon meal so when the meeting finally broke up they headed directly to the cafeteria. As they waited they were joined in the line by Jack Myers and the President, John McCleary. Those two elbowed their way into the line with no apologies to anyone. As soon as they were seated Jack opened the conversation by saying, "I don't want to hear the word no from either of you this evening. There are changes coming which will be greater than anything we have had to deal with since the virus struck. If Jack Wilson was still alive he would agree with me one hundred percent. This country is going to need the abilities of you two men more than at any time in the past. You cannot refuse what we are going to ask of you." Brendon spoke up at this point. He said, "That is a good speech Jack, but what does it mean? Chris and I have devoted most of our adult lives serving this county in some capacity. Right now we are trying to start a business to support our families and we don't have the time to devote to another job." Jack replied to this by saying, "At the risk of offending you, your business at this point is unimportant. Over the next ten years the population of this country is going to increase by at least threefold. We need to have people in place to insure the newcomers do not bury our culture, subvert our government or change our standards of acceptable behavior. The majority of these new people will be of white, European descent but there will be a substantial number of African, Asian and Arabic people as well. We have to be certain that all of them are greeted and treated the same. Chris that will be your job. Brendon your area of concern will be transportation. Our roads are in terrible condition and we do not have a railroad system. Both of those things must change and soon. You will be paid reasonable salaries and if you wish, you can base your offices in Perry so you won't need to move again. You can expect to do a lot of traveling so make sure your flying skills stay sharp. The government will furnish you with suitable aircraft though I am sure you own mechanics will want to do the maintenance." Chris and Brandon could only sit and stare straight ahead. Their meals arrived and remained untouched. Finally, John broke the silence. He told them their lack of refusal appeared to be a yes and that one day the country would thank them. John told them their new jobs would be ranked at the Cabinet level and they could be removed from office only by the President and only for a criminal offense. The jobs would most likely occupy them for the rest of their working lives. Chris and Brendon had planned for a 7:00 am departure on the 4th. They were asked to delay that time and attend a four hour meeting in which the details of their jobs would be outlined. Neither man ate their meal which had grown cold. They each picked up a sack lunch and retired to their room. In the privacy of their room Brendon asked if they were really going to accept the positions. Chris replied, "I suppose we must, otherwise Jack Wilson is going to come roaring out of his grave. That act would destroy the rose Martha planted and we certainly don't want to upset that sweet little old lady."

The next morning, Chris and Brendon were given a brief sketch of their duties and told they would have almost dictatorial powers and unlimited funds to carry out those duties. Chris was to determine the order in which people were to be moved and where they would be settled. Brendon was tasked with putting a working rail system in order and preparing the highway system for increased use. They were asked to have a brief outline of their plans ready to submit to Congress and the President by

June 1st. As an afterthought they were told to bring Hans Wilhelm to Montgomery even if it meant kidnapping him. He was still the Chief Justice of the Supreme Court, his wisdom and judgment were going to be sorely needed for the next two or three years. He could then retire but not before.

Chris and Brendon arrived home in late afternoon. After supper Brendon and Phoebe drove the ATV to the Weddle house and a conference was held. The men briefly explained what they were being asked to do and were met with silence. Chris, suspecting the reason for the silence was quick to add that the jobs would not require moving their homes again. He did add that it would require substantial travel for both himself and Brendon but that both of them would have their home offices in Perry. Both women smiled in relief and Phoebe told them all she had been afraid they were going to have the first real fight of their married life as she had no intention of ever moving her home again. Carol added a heartfelt amen and they began discussing locations for the offices. Carol recalled an office complex which had been built on the west side of Perry not long before the world ended. They agreed to inspect the place the next day and the meeting ended with coffee and dessert on the deck with the welcome song of the wolves ringing in the night.

Chapter 32 ----- 2134

On April 7 the Wolf Song community gathered at the shelter house for the monthly supper. For the first time the meat was not prepared by Chris or Brendon but by Brendon Jr. who had processed the ham, pork chops and sausage from start to finish. When it was acclaimed as up to the Hintz-Weddle standard Jr. stood to say thank you for the applause. While he was standing he added that in September there was going to be a Brendon III. He said it was an honorable name and he and Donna wished to see it perpetuated.

Chris and Brendon explained their new jobs and where their offices would be. Every one of the teen aged girls in the group offered to clean up the offices and the boys said they would pitch in to dispose of any garage or bones which needed to be removed. Now Chris Jr. asked for the floor and appeared quite nervous. This was unusual as he was normally a very self-assured young man. He told the group he was speaking for Craig, Aaron and George as well as himself. The boys had spent two days discussing what they, and, as a group could do to facilitate the founding of the new community which as going to be thrust upon them. They had talked at length with Uncle Pete and he had agreed to be their advisor and chief administrator until they were old enough and experienced enough to assume complete control of the operation. Even with Pete's oversight and guidance they would not proceed without the total approval from both sets of parents. Their plan was to start up the composite plant in Dallas Center again. Much of the machinery could be salvaged from defunct plants within seventy-five miles of Dallas Center. The rest could be fabricated from the plans and drawings to be found in

Montgomery. "We would ask you parents to consider and discuss this before you give us your answer," Chris Jr. said as he sat down to a stunned silence. Pete broke the silence by standing and announcing that he had already talked with Jake Brown, who was no relation to Pete, who was one of the best organizers and administrators Pete had ever worked with or for. Jake had agreed to come to Iowa and take an active part in the startup if it was decided to proceed. After much discussion the parents gave their consent to the proposed endeavor. There were reservations by the adults but at the same time they felt with Pete and Jake supervising there was a good chance of success.

A phone call, via the short wave radio, was placed to Lance in Montgomery. Lance was enthusiastic about the project and said he would send four of his most experienced supervisors to assist in the assembly and startup of the Dallas Center plant. Lance added that they had been making spares for many critical parts specific to production of the composite and that the parts would save considerable time and effort. With the issue of the composite plant settled Chris and Brendon moved into their new offices and began to formulate a plan for establishing railroad and highway systems. They decided that initially they would rehabilitate four east-west and four north-south lines with highways roughly parallel to the railroads. They proposed recruiting South Africans and Zimbabaweans with experience in all phases of railroad and highway work for the first two years of the project. With the ten ships promised by the South Africans carrying five hundred people and each ship making two trips per year, twenty thousand people could be transported the first two years. Perhaps one third of that number would be workers. The rest would be spouses, children, the old and people to provide services such as medical and food preparation. The operation would strain the system with regard to housing and food supply. It would require the participation of everyone already settled and in turn the newcomers would have to assist with the following waves of immigrants as they arrived. The proposal advocated starting with the northern route from Council Bluffs to Baltimore and at the same time work south to north from Mobile to Detroit. This would enable them to locate the newcomers in areas of Iowa and Alabama which already contained established communities, thus making the food and housing issues easier to manage. The summer passed quickly with four ship loads of highway and railroad workers arriving and being put to work immediately. The accompanying people were settled in the Perry and Montgomery areas and many of them managed to get late gardens planted. Any home or farm not set up with a solar system was given a wind turbine of sufficient size to heat and light the premises. The South Africans announced they had ten more ships being refurbished for transporting immigrants. These ships were larger and were capable of carrying one thousand to fifteen hundred people per trip.

Chapter 33 ----- 2132

Progress on the Dallas Center plant proceeded at a quicker pace than anyone could have predicted. Machinery was found and trucked in from all over Iowa. Some smaller machines were found in Illinois and the plant in Montgomery was turning out spare parts for the machines specific to the production of the composite.

In the middle of the summer George announced that he wanted to withdraw from the group. Both he and Martha wanted to study highway and bridge construction and eventually create their own company. It meant the two would have to return to Montgomery for the classes they would need. Phoebe wept at the prospect of losing part of her family but assured the two that this would always be their home and that they could return any time they chose. Brendon Jr. told George that his horses would receive the best care and would be his whenever he came for them. Rooms were found near the University complex in Montgomery and in August the two were flown to Montgomery and their class schedules arranged.

Both the highway and railroad crews made better progress than had been anticipated. I-80 had been in sporadic use for years all the way from Council Bluffs to the Chicago area. Areas requiring major repairs were already known so progress was rapid. The rail work was slower as the crews were required to make a walking inspection of every mile of track. The crews found an ample supply of rolling stock in Omaha and Council Bluffs and soon had the diesel electric engines operating. They converted passenger cars to bunk cars and used multiple dining cars to insure there were no long waits at meal time. Any trains stalled on the tracks were pushed on to sidings to be dealt with later. Any wrecked or damaged units were simply lifted and rolled out of the way. When winter shut down the work the crews were across Iowa and well into Illinois. After the first summer there was a general feeling that by increasing the number of work crews the initial rail lines and highways would be completed in another year and a half. As areas filled up the local communities would need to take responsibility for maintaining the systems and expanding them to include local roads and rail lines. During the fall and early winter several more ship loads of workers arrived in Mobile and were immediately moved to Houston, New Orleans and Jacksonville. With the mild southern weather they began working north on both the highways and railroads. Their final destinations were Minneapolis, Chicago and New York City. Crews were also started east from Houston with Jacksonville as their goal.

The Halsey and Discovery were being restocked with supplies needed for another long voyage. It had been decided to send ships to Australia to see if the virus free zone across South American and Africa extended to Australia as well. The Discovery had touched on the north and east coasts of the continent in 2116 but had turned away from New Zealand before reaching the latitudes later found to be virus free in the two continents to the east.

Chapter 34 ----- 2135

It had been decided to settle the first arrivals from South Africa along the I-65 corridor between Mobile and Detroit plus along I-80 east from Council Bluffs. The newcomers began arriving in February and were encouraged to stay in the south. They simply didn't comprehend the severity of mid-western winters. Those who insisted they wanted to go north were placed in temporary housing and told they could go north in March and April when the weather abated. Every industry related to rebuilding was working to capacity and most were begging for an increase in materials production. Two steel mills in Birmingham were collecting every scrap of iron or steel they could gather without being accused of theft. They were also crying for the Minnesota iron ore fields to be put into production. The three young men involved in restarting the composite plant took notice of the increased demand for their product and immediately began making plans to open two more plants. One plant to be located in Lexington, Kentucky and the other in Pittsburg. The advisors to the boys listened to their plans and gave their approval. The search for usable facilities and equipment was started immediately and everyone involved was soon working twelve to sixteen hour days. All three of the boys were taking flying lessons but would not be permitted to fly their own planes until they were eighteen. Each of them was supplied with a four seat, single engine plane which had been refurbished by Rascal and Jib. Those two had more or less retired but insisted on caring for the planes being used by the Wolf Song family. The pilots were selected by Pete and firmly instructed about flying in questionable weather. The boys were also given firm orders not to question the judgment of the pilots.

By June, the influx of newcomers had increased to a veritable flood. A belt along highway I-80 and extending for thirty miles north and south stretched across Iowa and Illinois. This belt hummed with activity such as had not been seen in over twenty-five years. The town of Dawson, now named New Home, was showing signs of coming to life again. A total of fifteen homes had been built and more were in the planning stages. Many of the new arrivals had come from small communities and they preferred the environment even if it meant commuting to work some distances away.

One enterprising young couple opened a small store which carried basic food and household items. Business was brisk and they soon found themselves expanding the store. What they were not aware of was that they had chosen a corner occupied by a general store which had been destroyed by fire almost two hundred years in the past. Four farming families heard of the plans of Chris and Brendon for a seed and nursery operation which had been abandoned when they had been given their present jobs. The families inspected the land and the seedling trees already planted. They then went to Chris and Brendon and requested permission to move onto the land and restart the operation. They offered to pay for the seedlings when the farm became a paying and profitable operation. Chris and Brendon gave their approval and told the newcomers to take the trees as a welcoming gift. The families consisted of four brothers named Kruger, their wives and a total of six children between them. Their family had been in South Africa for more than two hundred fifty years and the move had been a traumatic one for all of them. Chris and Brendon invited all of them to attend the September Wolf Song supper. Little Linda Ann who had apparently appointed herself as the spokesperson of the group made a short speech welcoming all the Krugers to Iowa. She finished by asking them to stay until her woofies had sung their nightly lullaby for them. Jonathon announced that he and Mavis were moving back to the community. He told the group that the primary purpose of the move was so Phoebe could fulfill her duties of being a full time grandmother to twins and triplets. This of course brought

Phoebe to the verge of tears and for a change she didn't have a word to say in reply. Craig and Janis Marie, who hadn't been an arms-length apart all evening, announced they were going to be married as soon as Janis turned eighteen. Hans announced his retirement effective the first of the year. He had found a fifty year old Cheyenne man who had been a graduate law student when the world ended. This man, named Patrick Whitehurst, had been working with Hans and would take over the practice when Hans retired. Hans was in Iowa visiting and needed to return to his duties as Chief Justice in two days. Before the wolf song chorus began Linda Ann was nestled, half asleep, in her Grandpa Hans's lap but stirred enough to tell everyone to be quiet and listen to the lullaby. The Krugers were impressed with the meeting and vowed they were going to start their own version as soon as they were well settled. Gene, the oldest of the brothers, commented that they would most likely have to settle for a coyote chorus as they had heard no wolves at their new homes.

With the onset of winter the highway and railroad crews were all moved south. By spring they planned to have four east-west plus four north-south routes for both the highways and railroads open and ready for traffic. They were already discussing plans to open another north-south route as well as one more east-west one. They intended to wait until the first eight lines were completed before starting on the last two

Chapter 35 ----- 2136

January was a sad month for the New Home community. Sven who was eighty was found one sunny afternoon sitting on the ground, leaning against one of his beloved apple trees with a pair of pruning shears in his lap. It appeared as if he had stopped to rest and had simply passed to the next life without a struggle. Two weeks later Rachael went to bed one night and didn't wake in the morning. Mary Lou and Gordon vowed they would make the orchard one of which Sven would be proud. Brendon III who had been born with a defective heart passed away just two days after Rachael. The entire community was in mourning and especially Phoebe who had held and tended to the baby almost every day of his life. All of this grief was compounded by the return of the lung ailment Carol had incurred in 2106. She was often short of breath and Brad had equipped her with a portable oxygen bottle which she carried at all times. Chris was terrified at the prospect of losing the woman in search of whom he had walked thousands of miles. He had always envisioned the two of them growing old together as they sat on the deck looking out over the river while holding hands. Carol assured him she planned to be around at least long enough to see his hair turn as gray as her own. At age fifty his hair was the same brown it had been at thirty. His beard did show some gray if he went two days without shaving.

In April, George and Martha sent word that they would be home to stay in August. They were currently enrolled in the final engineering classes offered in Montgomery and were anxious to come home and launch their careers.

In July, Craig and Janis were married. Janis became pregnant almost immediately and two sets of prospective grandparents were extremely pleased. The three young men involved in opening the composite plants agreed that Craig should take over the Dallas Center plant, Aaron would have the Lexington facility and Chris Jr. would go to Pittsburg. Two mothers were not happy to have their sons move so far away but there was no escaping that issue if they were going to operate three facilities. The boys pointed out that it was no more than a two hour flight from either city.

While the original estimate of the people who would move to the U.S. was one hundred thousand; that number was exceeded in the less than two years of the migration. People were still lining up to board the ships in South Africa and Zimbabwe. There was more than enough land for the newcomers but they system was taxed to the limit to feed, clothe and provide adequate housing. More than a few wanted to settle in Kansas, Nebraska and the Dakotas to raise wheat and other grains. Others were opting for Colorado, Wyoming and Montana to start sheep and cattle ranches. This of course put a burden on the highway and railroad renovation crews to provide a means to get the grain and livestock to the eastern markets. The Halsey and Discovery returned to Mobile in October with much exciting news. There was indeed a virus free zone extending across the continent of Australia which contained a population of some two million people. For the most part they were faring very well and displayed no interest in moving to North America. There were a few individuals who had expressed a desire to move but the general opinion was that they were simply looking for the excitement a change would bring.

The only major event of the voyage occurred as they were about to enter the harbor at Brisbane. The Halsey was trailing the Discovery by perhaps three miles when the Discovery turned around the southern point of Moreton Island and disappeared from view. Within minutes the men on the Halsey began to hear what sounded like gun fire from large weapons of three or four inch caliber. Moments later the Discovery appeared around the point traveling at flank speed. The skipper was on the radio and announced that they had been fired upon by an unidentified vessel. The first salvo had destroyed his forward gun and the stern mount was inoperable. He had two dead crewmen and another three wounded. The Halsey went to full speed and her guns prepared for firing. On turning the point of the island they spotted a small ship sitting broadside no more than a mile away. There were instant puffs of smoke as two five inch deck guns fired at the same time. The first salvo splashed well astern of the Halsey which turned to unmask both of her turrets of twin three inch guns. The order was given to fire and the first salvo from a U.S. Navy ship in many years was loosed. The first rounds landed short but all four shells from the second salvo struck the other ship amidships. They must have struck an explosives' storage area for the center of the ship blew up and she broke in half. In minutes the two halves both sank and nothing remained except debris and a few men floundering in the water. The Halsey moved in with the intention of picking up survivors. When they arrived at the scene they were greeted by the sight of a massive school of sharks savaging the men in the water. It was over before a boat could be lowered. There were no survivors. A lookout reported that a signal light was blinking from shore. The message was short. It simply said the ship which had been sunk was a pirate vessel and the people on shore were friendly and wished to speak with ship's captain. The Halsey anchored in Brisbane Harbor with her guns trained on the waterfront and all of her men heavily armed. The Discovery circled the Halsey but did not anchor. After an hour a twenty foot motor launch flying a white flag and carrying six men set out from the waterfront and approached the Halsey. As the launch neared the Halsey the six men could see the rails of the ship were lined with heavily armed men in full combat gear. The launch hove to some distance away and a man stood up in the bow with a megaphone. The man shouted, "I am Jason Whitestone, the mayor of Brisbane, none of us are armed and we pose no threat. May we come aboard?" After carefully scanning the launch the skipper ordered the boarding stairs lowered and the men in the launch were told to come aboard. Over the next hour the history of the pirate ship was told. She was a former Coast Guard ship which had been in the process of being refurbished with the idea of using her to explore the southwest Pacific to search for possible survivors. When the refit was ninety percent complete a group of twenty or so men boarded her one night. They killed the half dozen caretakers on board and sailed out of Brisbane Harbor. Within the next year they had recruited another twenty men, mostly from the dives in the small towns along the east coast. They had attacked and sunk two small ships which carried goods and people up and down the coast. She had even sailed into Brisbane Harbor and sunk a ship which was being armed and fitted out to combat the piracy. The small towns along the coast lived in fear of seeing the ship appear off of their waterfront. The well-armed pirates came ashore and took what they wanted in the way of food and other goods. They kidnapped women who, when they were tired of them, were simply thrown overboard to the ever present sharks. At the present time there were crews in Sydney working to prepare two fast ships to patrol the coast. The Discovery came alongside and was tied up to the Halsey. On seeing the damage to the Discovery, Mayor Whitehurst suggested the ship be brought into port and repaired. He stressed that there would be no cost for the repairs as a reward for ridding the coast of the pirates. The ships spent three weeks in port as crews worked around the clock to repair the Discovery. It was decided to send four representatives with the ships to discuss future trade with the U.S. The Australians were in need of all types of grain except rice. They also needed cotton cloth. In return they had a surplus of rice and an electronics industry desperate to find a market. The four representatives would have full authority for setting the terms of trading. The Australians were flown to Montgomery and were soon meeting with U.S. officials discussing trade. A program was soon underway at all of the Gulf and Atlantic seaports to find and start rehabilitating ships suitable for the voyage to Australia and back. The same process was taking place in Australia at the same time. Both countries were also putting small warships back in service. They were determined there would be no recurrence of the pirate situation such as had happened in Australia.

Chapter 36 ----- 2140

Over an eight year period the originally estimated one hundred thousand immigrants for South Africa had become an actual total of more than seven hundred fifty thousand and they were continuing to arrive, in lesser numbers to be sure, but a steady stream with no end in sight.

The newcomers, for the most part, settled along the corridors formed by the recently opened railroad and highway systems. In some areas of Iowa and Alabama where the Americans had settled, the population in small towns and cities plus the rural areas rose to what it had been in the days before the virus. Of course there were still vast areas with little or no population which would remain that way for many, many years. For several years there had been talk of moving the Capital from Montgomery to a city closer to the center of the population. Congress finally agreed on the city of Nashville. It was well served by the railroad and highway systems and had a first class airport close to the city. As they were contemplating these changes they also altered the rules for terms in public office. The new rules would limit a person to two four year terms in office rather than the current three year terms. The residency requirement for full citizenship and voting rights was lowered from ten years to five. These changes were submitted to the Supreme Court which ruled them legal and constitutional. The changes were then submitted to the voters in the form of a referendum and were approved by a substantial majority. A team of surveyors and civil engineers was sent to Nashville with the assigned task of locating a suitable location for the government campus. The team settled on the site of a long abandoned golf course on the west bank of the Cumberland River. Surveying began immediately and a panel of urban planners was assembled to lay out the arrangement of the new seat of government. With the change in the citizenship laws it meant the newcomers would soon outnumber the native born Americans at the polls. There were questions as to what changes this might bring in regard to laws and public opinion.

Life in the Wolf Song community had undergone drastic changes. The young people who had been born in the teens were now adults, most of them were now married with children of their own. Some lived as close as the newly named village of New Home which had grown to more than four times its original population. Richard (Jib) Jackson had been elected mayor and it appeared as if it might be a lifetime job. There were now a half dozen businesses along the old main street. A two hundred year old tradition, of the stores remaining open until nine on Wednesday night, was started again. It quickly became a social as well as a shopping event and much serious courting went on among the young people.

The Wolf Song suppers continued but with most of the young people living some distance away the suppers were not as well attended as in the past. Phoebe in particular was distressed over the lack of little ones to cuddle and coddle with treats. Chris Jr. always made an effort to drive up from Dallas Center with his wife and year old son who had been named Dallon Elliott. Judith or as she was called, Judy, told Jr. several times, "You Yanks have a funny way of speaking but you certainly have family and neighborhood bashes." Jr. replied that was because they were all family. Judy asked about the inclusion of the Cheyenne in the extended family saying that sort of thing didn't happen in her native Zimbabwe. Chris Jr. dug out the written accounts his father's and Melinda's walk from Wyoming to Mount Vernon plus his mother's trek out of Mexico. After reading the journals Judy's only comment was, "such people, I am honored to be considered a member of this family." Both Kathie and Pearl had stayed with their plans of becoming doctors. Kathie had specialized in Pediatrics and Pearl in Geriatrics. With three other doctors they had opened a clinic in Fort Dodge. They claimed that as a group they could provide medical care from the birth to the end of life. The two women had never married and both said they simply didn't have time for a husband and family. At age twenty-five they joked with each other about being the old maid sisters of the extended Wolf Song family. House calls for doctors were a thing of the past but both insisted on being called for any medical needs in the family. Hans who was now eighty-three, Rascal who was seventy-two and Martha who was seventy all refused to see any doctor other than Pearl. This resulted in many hurried trips from Fort Dodge to Wolf Song and New Home. The teachers, Frank and Nadine Murphy, who had been with the group for so many years, vowed when they retired that Pearl was to be their doctor. Martha had moved to a large house in New Home built by Rascal and Jib. She opened a new nursery and daycare center and soon had more little ones than she could care for. Letha, with her love for children, moved in with Martha and became a partner in the operation. There was one black cloud which hovered over the community. Carol's lung condition had worsened and she now required oxygen on a full time basis. She had a machine, which generated oxygen, and with a long flexible hose she was able to move around the house and even move outside to sit on the deck. To go beyond the reach of the machine meant strapping on an oxygen bottle. Carol had very little stamina so she spent most of her time sitting. Linda Ann, who was now fourteen and Chris had taken over all of the household tasks. Carol, who had always been a self-sufficient individual, was devastated that her daughter was losing what should have been fun filled teen years to care for an invalid mother. Linda tried to reassure her mother that she had the rest of her to have fun, for now, caring for Carol was the most important thing in her life. Chris lived in constant dread of losing this woman who was more important to him than life itself. The team of doctors who were treating Carol told them the oxygen would keep her alive for four to seven years. After that the lung function would deteriorate to the point where it would not support life. Chris was distraught but Carol reminded him she had promised to be around at least until his hair was as gray as her own. So far there was no hint of gray on his head.

Chapter 37 ----- 2145

Much had changed in Iowa over the past five years. Most of the immigrants were now counted as citizens with full voting right. With a population approaching one hundred seventy-five thousand it was one of the most populous states in the fourteen state union. Rather than try to rehabilitate Des Moines a new capital was established in Ames and construction of the capital campus would go on for a number of years. Iowa State University was reopened and offered a full range of college classes including medicine. It turned out that the South African immigrants were as conservative as any Iowa farmer from 2050 so there was very little movement to change laws or customs.

One June day in 2143 a man of about fifty-five years walked into the office Chris maintained in Perry and asked if he might speak with Chris. When asked about the subject he replied that it was personal and he would prefer that Chris make the decision whether the matter became public knowledge. After the secretary conferred with Chris the stranger was shown into his office. The man offered his hand and said his name was Dr. Jerry Doolittle. When the University opened in Ames he would be a full professor of surgery with a specialty in organ transplants. He handed Chris a bulging folder while telling him it contained a history of his education and his career as a surgeon. In a rush of words Jerry went on to say the journals of Chris and Carol were virtually required reading for all of the newcomers and it would give him great personal pleasure to be of service to the principal founders of the new state of Iowa. Chris was taken aback by being named as a founder of Iowa but he recovered enough to ask what that service might be. Jerry replied that he knew of Carol's condition, it was public knowledge after all, and he wanted to perform a lung transplant. He stated that he had performed the operation over twenty times and the only failure had been a young man whose heart had been damaged by a bout of Rheumatic Fever as a child. There was no longer an issue of tissue rejection as a new serum provided lifetime immunity with one injection. It was certainly not a routine surgery but he had been highly successful with it in the past. At the present time he had a young woman on life support at the hospital in Ames. She had been struck in the head by a falling tree limb two days ago and suffered massive brain damage. There was no hope of recovery and her parents wanted the machines turned off as soon as possible. They already had recipients for the heart, kidneys and corneas. If Carol agreed to the procedure the team of surgeons would do all four operations simultaneously.

Chris had put a large beef roast on the grill that morning. He called Linda and asked her to prepare enough vegetable and salad to feed a guest he was bringing home for supper. Jerry followed Chris and they drove into the parking area to find Carol sitting on the deck listening to Rock & Roll music almost two hundred years old. Chris suggested they go into the house so all four of them could sit at the table and talk. Linda Ann was only seventeen but she was treated as an adult because she had taken on the responsibilities of an adult. Chis placed the folder holding Jerry's credentials on the table and told the two women that Jerry was going to present them with some information and how they responded to that information would be left for Carol to decide. By the time Jerry finished speaking all three of the Weddles were openly weeping. Carol finally regained her composure enough to day, "I have been dreaming of this day for six years and never thought it would ever happen. Can we start tomorrow?" Jerry told her if she checked in the hospital tomorrow for some tests they could do the surgery in three days.

Now, two years later, Carol was back to the lithe athletic form which had enabled her to walk out of Mexico those many years ago. George and Martha, on their return from school in Montgomery had, with assistance from Brendon and Chris opened a construction and engineering firm. They had an office in Perry plus an equipment yard outside of New Home. Brendon, who had not forgotten the old covered bridges in Madison County, made a trip to look at them again. They had continued to deteriorate and were in deplorable condition. Brendon finagled a contract with the State to renovate the bridges. The contract went to the new Hintz Construction firm. The bulk of the contract was contingent on the timely and satisfactory completion of one bridge chosen at random. Inspection of the bridge and surveying of the site commenced immediately. The composite plant in Dallas center geared up to produce panels, beams and pilings for the bridge. The job went quickly and the finished bridge was pronounced as exceeding expectations and the young firm was told to proceed with the remaining bridges.

While working with the bridge crew Martha met and soon fell in love with one of the engineers. He was a South African named Patrick Willson. During the wedding preparations George was introduced to Patrick's sister, Penelope, and another romance soon blossomed.

With Carol's health restored, Linda announced she was going to Ames and study law. She had always admired her Grandpa Hans and hoped someday to take his seat on the U.S. Supreme Court. On hearing Linda's statement Hans broke down and wept openly. He had never had children of his own and Linda had become his pet among the children of the Wolf Song and New Home community. Hans even contacted the Dean of the Law School in Ames and told him to take very good care of this special young woman.

For the first time in thirty years Chris and Carol found themselves alone in their home. Chris had been allowed to resign his position as head of the Resettlement Program. The influx of newcomers had slowed to a trickle so the details could be handled by the office staff and a soon to be named manager.

Brendon also requested and was relieved from his duties with the railroad and highway projects. He was soon drafted by George and Martha as an unofficial advisor for their construction firm. He also rejoined his son in the farming operation. They added three hundred twenty acres of land to their holdings plus an additional ten cows to the milking herd.

A brisk trade had developed between the four continents. Everything from electronics to medicine to bananas was shipped. An engineering group was formed to study the feasibility of re-opening both the Panama and Suez Canals to shorten shipping distances.

In Charleston, S.C. a three hundred fifty foot destroyer was taken out of the moth ball fleet and refitted for duty. The ship was given the number NBB-2 and renamed the Admiral Nimitz. The plan was to send the new U.S. Navy across the Indian Ocean to visit India, Sri Lanka and the nations of Southeast Asia. At the same time two small, armed ships would investigate the Mediterranean basin and the coast of Europe. Eventually they wanted to retrace the original route of the Discovery in Asia and the Southwest Pacific. Australia was going to undertake this part of the plan and was working on ships with which they would carry it out. With the launch into a high equatorial orbit of three communication satellites there had been a restoration of television, telephone and computer service. It was all wireless and served to draw the residents of all four continents closer together. The influx of so many spurred the economy while at the same time, deer, elk and coyotes which had been a common sight in yards and gardens became a rarity. The wolf serenade, so cherished by the residents of Wolf Song and New Home, all but disappeared. Occasionally a single animal could be heard but now it seemed to be a lonely, haunting cry.

Time and age were beginning to catch up to the original survivors. Hans Wilhelm who was eighty-eight sat down for his usual afternoon nap one day and passed away in his sleep. The teachers, Frank and Nadine Murphy, who had been with the group from the beginning, both died within three weeks of each other. Rascal could walk only with great difficulty and using two canes. His primary means of locomotion was an electric wheel chair which had been assembled by Jib. Jib had added a bright colored sun shade to the chair and Rascal made a circuit of New Home almost every day. He had become something of a grandfather figure in the community. The children had developed the habit of giving him gifts, mostly flowers ranging from dandelions to roses plucked from some unsuspecting gardener's prize bush. The smaller children often presented him with pretty or odd colored stones they had picked up. Rascal treasured the stones and displayed them on a table in his home. Chris had finally turned gray. Carol teased him about it, telling him with as many grandchildren as they had it was time he started looking the part. Kathie and Pearl had relented from their claim of being too busy for marriage and both married men who were partners in the practice in Fort Dodge. They along with four other doctors moved their offices to New Home and became closely associated with the hospital and clinic in Perry. They were not aware of the fact but they were the first doctors to have an office in the New Home area in over two hundred years.

Chapter 38 ----- 2150

On a warm May afternoon, Carol was sitting on the deck with a glass of lemonade. She was babysitting two grandchildren who at the moment were down for their afternoon naps. She had been musing about the past and reached the conclusion that at age sixty-eight she no longer had the stamina to keep up with a pair of four year olds she one had at age forty or even fifty. No that she minded, it was always one of the highlights of her day when one or two of the little ones were left with her rather than Letha and Martha's day care. Usually Chris was on hand to help but today he had been called to Linden to arbitrate a dispute over access to the river. A strange van pulled into the parking area and Carol noticed it had dog boxes built in on one side. A middle aged man jumped out and ran around to the passenger side where he began a very elderly lady get out. It was obvious she didn't want help as she kept brushing his hand away from her elbow. Carol walked out, turned off the power fence and opened the gate. The man introduced himself as Frank and told Carol they had met once, twenty-five years ago. He was the one who had taken over the predator control business when Hans had put on a suit and went back to the practice of law. The elderly lady looked faintly familiar but Carol could not put a name to the face. The lady called Carol by name and told her she had once said they might meet again. She continued by saying, "It is many mile and many years since we were in Palm Springs but here we are again." The name Palm Springs triggered Carol's memory and she said, "You are Lisa Meyers and I have never forgotten your kindness." Frank told the women he needed to go home as he had chores waiting for him. He told Lisa to call him, no matter the hour, and he would return to take her home. Carol suggested that Lisa spend the night as Chris would be home late and would surely want to meet her. She added they could find something to serve as a nightie and could do some laundry if need be. Lisa readily agreed and added that she needed to have a serious conversation with Chris. Lisa then asked if it would be possible to include Brendon Hintz in the conversation when Chris returned. Carol told her they would do better than that. Carol said she would call for a "seniors only" community supper at her house. If need be she would tell the others it was an emergency so as to insure their attendance. She immediately put a ham on the spit then began preparing cherry pies. Word of the pies would insure the attendance of both Brendon and Pete. Carol called Phoebe and asked them to come and if Phoebe would please bring potato salad. Carol decided to include the Sweets and a phone call was made. Melinda who loved the family gatherings readily agreed. Pete accepted and said he would even wash dishes if he could have a second piece of cherry pie. Carol told him she would make an extra pie just for him and he could take home what he didn't eat for supper she added that he would not have to wash any dishes to pay for it.

As the guests arrived they were introduced to Lisa. When she met Brendon he was given an extra-long hug and a kiss on the mouth. When Chris, who was the last to arrive, came in, he was given the same greeting as Brendon had received. As the group ate there was a lively round of conversation which centered on children, grandchildren and the prospect of great-grandchildren. Lisa tried to take in every word of the conversations but there were just too many names to remember. During a lull in the talk Lisa remarked that when supper was over she had a story of her own she would like to share with them. Finally, Carol told everyone who wanted it to get coffee or lemonade and they would listen to Lisa's story.

Chapter 39 ----- 2150

isa's Story: I am ninety-five years old. My birth name was Lisa Wordworth and I was born and grew up in the San Francisco area. I was very independent so I never married or had children. At age twenty-five I started a home security business which thrived and which enabled me to take care of my parents. Both of them suffered from poor health all of their adult lives. From the time I was thirty they both required live-in help to manage day to day. My business provided the funds needed to pay for that care. They had both been in wheelchairs when the end came in 2106. I was in Palm Springs on that day for a business meeting and when I realized I was alone I walked and drove back to San Francisco. I found my parents sitting next to each other in their back yard. This was three weeks after the day the world ended so you can imagine the condition of their bodies. I wrapped both of them in blankets then dug a grave with a garden shovel and buried them together. The couple who had been caring for my parents was inside the house so I closed it up tight and went to my own place which was only about two miles away. I stayed there for about three months although I actually lost track of the time. I started having disturbing dreams. I often dreamed my name was Myers and I began using that as my name. I loaded a small utility van with my must keep possessions and drove to Palm Springs. I passed on through and finally stopped in Indio. I found a small, solar powered, two bedroom house and settled in. There was already a slow steady trickle of survivors drifting in from the desert and from the north so there were a few neighbors. The dreams continued with frequent referenced to Iowa. There were other words and place names which were never clear and which

I could never remember the next day. After I had been there for six months or so I was sunbathing on the back deck when a man walked down the alley. He was wearing a small back pack and was burned dark brown from the sun. On seeing me he immediately dropped the pack, hopped the fence and began approaching me. By this time I was on my feet and edging towards the door. He stopped and looked me over then said I was a little old for his usual tastes but he would take what he could get today. I made it inside and slammed the sliding door on his hand as he reached for me. When he jerked his hand back I latched the door and retreated to the living room. I had a .40 caliber Colt pistol on the bookcase and I picked it up just as he threw a concrete block through the glass door. The man stormed into the living room where I showed him the pistol and told him he still had a chance to leave. He sneered, said I didn't have the nerve to shoot and lunged at me. I fired two shots and I think both of them went through his heart. He tried to speak but no words came and he was dead within seconds. I didn't know how or where to report the incident but I certainly was not going to stay in the house with a dead man in the living room. I then remembered a truck stop on the edge of Indio which someone had reopened for simple sandwiches and coffee. I drove there and found a half dozen people passing the time. One of them happened to be a former small town police officer. He followed me home, looked over the scene and told me not to worry about it. He would write a report and keep it on hand until some kind of law enforcement agency was established. He and another man helped me load my vehicle and we returned to the diner. One of the women offered me her extra bed until I decided where to live. After a week I decided to move to Palm Springs. Soon after that I was approached about a job with the area's unofficial police. A year later I found Carol waving at me from a bridge following her walk out of Arizona and Mexico. Fifteen years later a group of us walked and drove from California to Montgomery. When Frank decided to move back to Redfield from Montgomery I moved with him. Since that time I have been living in a one room cabin on his property. Frank and his wife take very good care of me and I lack nothing but family.

When the computer network had been restored last year I had begun a search for relatives. After stumbling upon the Weddle genealogy I had traced and tracked and finally discovered that six generations in the past my grandmother from that generation was sister to the grandfather of Chris and Brendon from that time. A hush fell over the group as the enormity of Lisa's statement hit them. Suddenly everyone was talking. Chris stood and held up his hand. When the group fell silent Chris welcomed Lisa to the family and said he had a surprise for her as well. He then told her of Jackie being a cousin one generation later than the rest of them. He then told the group to consider their uniqueness. Out of three hundred fifty million people in the U.S. at the time of the disaster only about thirty-five thousand had survived. What are the odds that four of those people would be blood relatives? When the talk settled back to a low murmur as if on cue, the wolf song began. Rather than the usual one or two animals it sounded as if the entire pack from years past had joined in. When there was a lull in chorus Lisa asked, "What is that? It is beautiful." Carol spoke up and told Lisa that it was the wolf song from which the little community took its name. "Wolf Song," repeated Lisa, "that is one of the words from my dreams I could never remember." Chris who had been huddled and whispering with Carol now spoke up. He told Lisa that seeing her take so much enjoyment from being with her cousins had given him an idea. He was having a three bedroom house built in New Home. Lisa stopped his speech and said, "New Home that is the other word I could never remember clearly." She then said, "Pardon me, get back to what you were saying we can come back to this later." Chris resumed by saying the house was only two weeks away from completion. He then said if Lisa liked the house and wanted to move to New Home it would be hers as long as she wanted. He added that when and if Lisa wanted a live in caretaker he and Carol would pay for that also. By now Lisa was in tears while both Carol and Melinda attempted to comfort her. When the tears finally stopped the aged lady wiped her eyes and said, "All those years of being alone and now look, I have three cousins close enough to touch and a large number of nieces and nephews to meet and I hope, spoil at least a little bit. I accept your offer without even looking at the house." Then as if having heard Carol say it she added, "You are a good man Mr. Weddle." Lisa went on to tell the group that after she had finally found her family through the genealogy charts she had felt compelled to legally change her last name from Wordworth to Myers. After making the change official the dreams had ceased and she felt much more at ease about who she was. When the next regular Wolf Song supper was held two weeks later everyone was present. Aaron and Craig had flown in with their families from Lexington and Pittsburgh. All of them wanted to meet the new found cousin and hear her story. Megan and Margaret were both married and both were pregnant so a fourth generation was about to be added to the family tree. Lisa who was actually a generation older than her cousins pointed out that fact and said if the twins didn't take too long to give birth there would be five living generations in the family. The younger family members were instantly taken with Lisa and somehow it was decided to just call her Gran rather than Auntie or cousin. The old woman had never been around a group of gregarious and happy young people and she reveled in her newly appointed role as Matriarch of the extended clan.

Chapter 40 ----- 2150

When most of America died in 2106 organized sports passed into history as well. There simply were not enough children and young people in any given community to form a single team let alone a league. One of the things brought to America by the immigrants from the other three continents was their love of the sport of Rugby. As soon as there was an adequate number of young and sometimes not so young men in an area a team was formed. Often, if it was an isolated area, the men just practiced or scrimmaged among themselves. Soon they were using busses to visit nearby teams or, where available, the railroads for longer trips. Within five years a professional league was formed and the U.S. had a new national sport. Old football stadiums were refurbished and the best players became local heroes. With the restoration of television service games were broadcast to the public. The broadcasts were limited to Saturday only. They were not allowed to interfere with the work week or with Sunday which was reserved for worship or meditation. Cricket was introduced also but for the most part it remained a local game. It just didn't have the same attraction as watching a couple of dozen burly men pummeling each other.

Chapter 41 ----- 2150

The information coming from the Discovery group was spotty but exciting. They had attempted to enter the Persian Gulf but had been fired on by shore batteries from both Oman and Iran. They had reversed course without returning fire and proceeded to the coasts of Pakistan and India. Here they found sizeable populations of survivors. The survivors were all of various Asiatic ethnic groups. It appeared that no one from any of the white races had survived. The peoples of both countries were friendly and expressed their desire to reopen trade with the Americans. To show their sincerity they loaded six tons of tea on the Discovery with the assurance they had warehouses bulging with more plus rice, spices and a new type of fine porcelain they had developed. In return they wanted medicines, anything of a technological nature and American grain, particularly corn, oats and soy beans. The two ships sent to Europe and the Mediterranean areas found no one in Europe except in LeHavre, France. There they found a population of some five hundred. These people were miners, their families and descendants. They had been employees in a very deep coal mine. They and their families lived four hundred feet under-ground for two months at the time then returned to the surface for a like amount of time. They had emerged from the darkness to find their world gone. They had survived by scavenging from the now dead civilization and growing huge gardens; exactly as the Americans had done. Every one of them expressed the desire to immigrate to the U.S. where there were other people. It was promised that a ship would be sent for them within two years. A short wave radio was left with them and several people were trained in its use.

Along the coast of North Africa several pockets of people were found. They numbered from ten thousand to upwards of seventy-five thousand with most of them located along the Nile River in Egypt. They were open to the idea of trade but had no desire to leave what had been their homeland for thousands of years.

In the Middle East they found a sizeable population, the vast majority of whom were of Arabic blood. In Israel there were perhaps fifty thousand Israelis. They were centered around Haifa and Acre surrounded by Arabs still determined, after centuries, to drive them into the sea. The Israelis had begun formulating plans to gather enough ships to transport all of them at one time and sail to North America which they assumed was now empty of people. When told there was a sizeable population and that the U.S. was still a country the Israelis asked if perhaps there was a state in the west where they could move as a people and be unmolested in their worship. It would not be their traditional homeland but they could make it so and finally be free of continuous warfare. When Jason Keltz, the President of the United States read this message and request he sat down and drafted a message to Congress. He requested that the currently unoccupied former state of Utah be renamed New Israel and set aside as the new homeland of the Jews. All laws of the U.S. were to be respected and obeyed. Anyone who wished to do so could apply for U.S. citizenship and hold dual citizenship in both countries. Any Native Americans found living in the area were to have their property rights respected and would be subject only to U.S. law. Transportation for the newcomers would be provided from the U.S. east coast to the western boundaries of Colorado and Wyoming. There was enough arable land within the boundaries of the new political entity to support several times the population expected to move into it. Congress took the President's message, chewed on it, tweaked and finally passed a very unique set of laws. It became known as the "New Israel Act" and contained a provision which would allow the residents to apply for statehood within the Union. It would require a two-thirds popular voted to be considered for admittance to the U.S. The act was unprecedented in every way and was immediately challenged in court. Because of its magnitude the case went directly to the Supreme Court. The Court ruled that although it was a new and radical concept there was nothing in the Constitution forbidding it. The government of Israel granted approval and plans were made to start moving the Israelis to America. Two more ships of the new Nimitz class were taken out of the moth ball fleet and a crash program started to put them back in service. Word was passed to the assailants of the Israelis that they were to be evacuated by the U.S. Any attack on them would be considered as an attack on U.S. forces and would be met with the full power of the American Navy. This was something of an empty threat as the U.S. Navy consisted of three small armed ships with two more being fitted for sea duty. In any case the sniping and mortar attacks ceased and an uneasy truce settled over Haifa and Acre. Twenty cargo ships were quickly adapted to carry people and began a nonstop shuttle between the ports of Acre and Norfolk. Within a year the exodus was complete. There were a few hundred people who refused to leave their native land. There was little doubt what their future held in store but hey were adamant about remaining in their homeland.

Most of the newcomers settled along the I-15 corridor. Irrigation systems were restored and the land bloomed in the areas which could be watered. There was much land and so few people that there were very few disputes over living space. These were quickly settled by a panel of Jewish elders. One major change was that American English was required in the schools. Students were required to be proficient in both oral and written English by the time they were in the 5th grade. In the beginning there was much vocal resistance to this rule but eventually the need for a common language overcame the reluctance to change. Hebrew was still spoken in the Synagogue and in many homes but English became the common language of New Israel.

Chapter 42 ----- 2151

In the Wolf Song and New Home communities major changes were in motion.

Chris, who had led the way, and the people of his generation were stepping aside. They were in their 60's and 70's with some pushing 80. The pilots among them had given up flying but there were enough capable pilots in the next generation to fly them anywhere they wanted to go. Chris, Carol and Melinda were approached by a publisher and asked to put their stories of their epic walks into book form.

The four composite plants were combined into a single corporation with Chris Jr., Craig, Aaron and Pete Brown's son Bill as the Board of Directors with the corporate headquarters located in Perry. They were discussing the feasibility of opening another plant in New Israel. The various highways traveled by Melinda and Chris on their walk from Wyoming to Washington had been designated the Sweet-Weddle Memorial route. Bronze plaques were to be installed every fifty miles on the route. The plaques would show a man, woman and two dogs walking towards a setting sun with the appropriate date on each plaque. There was also some discussion of marking Carol's route of her walk out of Mexico. There were two drawbacks to that plan. First was that the route was in a foreign country however disorganized that county might be at the moment. Second was that in forty plus years since the event it was probable that the jungle had reclaimed much of the route Carol had traveled.

There was a huge debate about the future of the Bison. There was much discussion and finally laws were passed which gave the animals' free range west of highway US 83 from the

Rio Grande to the Canadian border and west to the Rocky Mountains. People would be allowed to settle in this area but they could not erect fences extending more than one mile east and west or north and south and must have a gap at least two miles wide between fences. Residents would be allowed to harvest the animals for their personal use only. No commercial trading of hides or meat would be allowed. A troop of two hundred men were recruited who would attempt to herd all of the Bison east of US 83 into the area reserved for them. Native Americans would be allowed to take the animals needed for customary uses but not to sell or trade. The Bald Eagle, whose numbers had soared over the past one hundred fifty years, was still protected, except Native Americans could take them for traditional ceremonial use.

Following the events of 2106 a new problem had arisen in America. Many foreign animals had escaped from zoos and animal preserves. Most of them had gradually migrated to the warmer climate in the south and breeding populations were soon established. The three big cats from Africa and Asia had little fear of man and it was not unusual to see one ambling along a city street. The various deer and antelope melted into the countryside and returned to their natural lifestyle. The big animals such as the rhino, hippo and elephant found bountiful food supplies. Once the scattered individuals found other of their kind the herds thrived. As the Hippopotamus population grew that animal took over several rivers in Florida and southern Georgia. When man began to move back into the area the conflict began. Both lions and tigers soon discovered that a child was easier to catch and just as tasty as a deer or wild cow. The hippos became a serious hazard to fishermen and boaters and all-out war was declared. Leopards soon developed an affinity for mutton and veal so the spotted cat was added to the list of undesirables. Even the elephants came under fire as they began to ravage crops, vineyards and orchards. It was a conflict which would go on for years and because of the scattered population of man might never be completely resolved.

Chapter 43 ----- 2155

2154 and 2155 became known as the years of dying. It began with the passing of Lisa Myers who died just a few months short of her 100th birthday. Her death was soon followed by those of Rascal, Jib and Martha Wilson. In March of 2155 the deaths began again. Pete Brown was the first to go followed in less than two weeks by Jackie. Carol attributed Jackie's death to simple heartbreak. She just did not wish to continue her life without Pete.

After almost six months of continuous shock and mourning the extended Wolf Song family needed something to lift their spirits. At the April Wolf Song supper, that lift would be provided by the ever practical Phoebe. The group had been discussing the people they had lost over the past few months when Chris commented that all of the elders were now gone. Phoebe stood and began to speak, "I beg to differ with Chris, the elders aren't gone, they have just been replaced. As I look around this table I see canes and walking sticks several of you are using. All of us are gray haired and remember pre-disaster days. I want to establish a formal Board of Elders consisting of ten members. Two of those members are from the next generation following my own. Mavis, my daughter, was only a child when we came here but she rocked, changed and burped almost every baby born to our group. She also named this Wolf Song supper we have all come to treasure. Her husband Jonathon was instrumental in getting his people settled and integrated into our community. The other members would be Chris, Carol, Brendon, myself, Brad, Melinda, Molly MacDonald and Patty Jackson. I would suggest that the chairperson of this Board be Carol simply because she went through more than anyone else to get here. Think about this and perhaps at the next supper we can discuss and vote on it." When the talk resulting from Phoebe's proposal had died out Craig Allen and William, his mother Jackie had called him Billy, approached Chris and Brendon who were seated together. Craig placed a bulging folder between the two older men then told them to look through the contents and comment on what they saw. On top of the stack of papers were a dozen photographs of an airplane taken from several angles. After looking at the photos for several minutes Brendon was the first to speak. He said, "These pictures are all of the Ugly Bird, when and where were they taken? I don't recognize the background." Chris entered the conversation by saying, "That certainly looks like the Ugly Bird but it isn't. The landing gear is different, the wings are more swept and the vertical stabilizer has a different profile." Billie told Chris he was correct and very observant. This plane was essentially the same as the original Ugly Bird but was two generations later in the evolution of the aircraft. It had been discovered, sitting on jacks in the final assembly line in the long idle factory in Wichita. It lacked only engines to be ready for rollout. The same type of engines which had powered the original Ugly Bird were installed and the nose lengthened to accept a camera and thermal sensor. Craig and Billie had a plan. They wanted to repeat the flight of Chris and Brendon in 2126. Rather than a marathon flight of one day they planned to stretch it over four days with overnight stops in Yuma, Bellingham and Rapid City. This would give them time and opportunity to really look at the terrain they were flying over. Their plan was to invite Chris, Carol, Brendon, Phoebe, Brad and Melinda to go with them. They had intended to invite Pete and Jackie on the flight but that was not to be. Craig and Billie, after taking possession of the plane, had kept it hangared in Cedar Rapids in an effort to keep it a secret from the family elders. While keeping the plane hidden they had each managed to log over seventy-five hours of flight time and were comfortable with the idea of piloting the elders on the long flight which was tentatively planned for a mid-June date.

Chapter 44 ----- 2155

On June 13 the group which was going on the flight met at the airport at 5:00 a.m. In addition to the three couples and the two pilots there were two others; Brendon Jr.'s daughter Phoebe and Dallon who was the son of Chris Jr. were going as well. These two were going to act as stewards for the older couples. Both Brendon and Brad had become what somewhat unsteady on their feet. It was thought they might need assistance in moving about the cabin while in flight. They lifted off the runway at 6:30 a.m. and headed southwest. They flew at an altitude low enough that oxygen was not required. They crossed the corner of Nebraska and were soon over Kansas. Everyone was amazed at the large areas planted to crops consisting for the most part of wheat and corn. Of course the majority of the land was untilled and resembled the prairie of three hundred years in the past. Across western Kansas, Oklahoma and Texas they spotted numerous herds of cattle and several bands of horses. A number of small herds of Bison were seen. Just north of Dalhart, Texas they spotted a small Bison herd being followed by a wolf pack. The wolves were not chasing the herd but were following closely. Brendon surmised the predators were sizing up the herd to determine which animal would be the most vulnerable. As they crossed New Mexico Billie was piloting the plane. Melinda went forward and asked him if they could make a careful inspection of the Rio Grande valley between Albuquerque and Socorro. After the moves to the Midwest years ago there were some seventy-five of the Cheyenne people not accounted for. Billie flew the full distance between the two cities then reversed course and went low and slow in the other direction. They saw no sign of life except wild horses and cattle. They increased their altitude to eleven thousand feet, turned on the cabin oxygen and headed west. Across western New Mexico then southern Arizona there was little to see except mountains and desert. They were high enough that people would have been all but invisible and large animals would have been mere specks. As they approached Yuma Craig made radio contact and was assured the runway was clear and safe to use. A team had flown in the day before with food, fuel and two mechanics in case they were needed. The mechanics had been trained by Rascal and Jib and were every bit as devoted to Chris as the first two had been. The Yuma airport saw very little use but it had been operational for over ten years. Anyone headed for southern California flew into Yuma and traveled overland from there. There were rooms and showers waiting for the travelers who were soon sitting on a shaded patio drinking iced tea and discussing what they had seen that day. The next morning as the group was boarding the plane each of them was handed a large, heavy folder by Craig. Inside each folder was a series of the photographs taken by Brendon and Chris during their flight in 2126. The photos were superimposed over maps of the California coast as it existed prior to 2106. Many of the changes were evident at a glance. Today's flight and resulting pictures would allow them to see the changes since the first flight. They lifted off from Yuma and headed directly west toward San Diego. Except for being deserted with no signs of life San Diego appeared much as it had in the past. Beginning at about San Clemente there were many changes. Great masses of the coast were gone. In some places it appeared as if the shore had receded by as much as four or five miles. Offshore here were new islands which had been pushed up from the seabed. On some of the islands there was already a faint tinge of green where new vegetation was taking root. There were also large numbers of seabirds on and around the islands. When they arrived over Los Angeles it was gone. There was a strip about two miles wide along the coast which was perhaps three hundred feet high. Inland from that strip was a new bay which was ten to fifteen miles wide and which stretched forty to fifty miles north and south. At about where Long Beach should have been there was a half mile wide inlet to the new bay. It must have been in the middle of a tide change as they could see white water which was evidence of a rapid current through the inlet. They continued north and the San Francisco area appeared much as it did in the pictures taken by Brendon and Chris on their flight. San Francisco and the peninsula south to San Jose were gone. A detail which had been missed by Chris and Brendon was that the north tower of the Golden Gate Bridge was still standing. It was tilted precariously to the east but against all reason remained standing. They turned east then north and flew more or less up the crest of the northern California mountains where they could detect little or no change from the time their photos had been taken. When they crossed into Oregon, that changed in a dramatic fashion. What had been Crater Lake was now Crater Mountain and it was huge and still growing. They estimated the new height to be at least twelve thousand feet and still growing. There was no evidence left of the crater which had given the lake its name. They could see molten lava pouring out of the top and flowing down the flanks of the new mountain. As they continued north they saw very little sign of volcanic or seismic activity. Crossing over the stump of Mount Hood they could see that there had been a flow of new lava in the crater but at present it appeared to be inactive. Crossing the Columbia they continued up the crest of the Cascades. Flying over the southern Washington volcanoes they could see no apparent changes from the pictures taken by Chris and Brendon on their previous flight. The Mount Rainier area was completely hidden by dense cloud cover so they were unable to determine if there had been any recent changes in that former giant. In the north at Mount Baker there were a number of obviously recent lava flows. There were also several active steam vents spewing white clouds into the air. The flight time from Mount Baker was a matter of only a few minutes and the group was soon on the ground inspecting their rooms for the night. They gathered in a small dining room at the former motel where they would be staying. They were surprised at the number of people present in the area and asked their host where they had all come from and what they did to support themselves. They were told that people continued to filter in after the exodus to the Midwest. Many had migrated north from California and other individuals had drifted in from all over the west. There were now almost four thousand people in the area and they had been considering asking to join the new U.S. The locals were aware of the population growth in the eastern half of the country and the influx of people form Africa, South America and Israel. They had chosen to remain isolated but were in desperate need of medicine and clothing. There were farms in the northern part of the Skagit Valley which produced more food than was needed for the present population. There was only one bridge across the Skagit River still standing. That bridge was located at Hamilton. All of the others fell during the quakes which destroyed the Skagit River dams. Mount Vernon was a virtual ghost town. Much of the town had been taken down by the quakes and floods following the dam failures. One positive result of the destruction was the recovery of the salmon runs in the river and its tributaries. The travelers were treated to grilled salmon that evening. They were assured that it was fresh from the Nooksack River that morning. While they were eating Chris said he had a request to make. He added that the pilots had to be in complete agreement and the he would understand if they were reluctant to grant his wish. They had already flown many miles and had many more miles to cover just to get home. He asked if they would be willing to leave the passengers in Bellingham the next day while they took the plane and flew the length of the Columba and Snake Rivers or at least those portions within the boundaries of Washington. Chris wanted pictures of all of the dams on both rivers. Both Craig and Billie agreed. They said any of the passengers who wished to do so were welcome to make the flight with them. Only Chris and Brendon accepted. Brad and the three women opted to take a day off from flying.

Next morning they flew directly south. When they reached Bonneville there was nothing left of the dam except the structures near the north and south shores. Down river from the dam site stretched a rapids caused by rubble from the collapsed dam. They continued up the river then turned and followed the Snake

River to the site of the Hells Canyon Dam. As with the Columbia dams every single dam on the Snake was now rubble, causing rapids downstream. Reversing course they flew back down the Snake then turned north and followed the Columbia to the Canadian border. Again there was not a single dam spanning the river. Even giant Grand Coulee was gone. There was a gap of perhaps five hundred feet in the center. The structures on both sides of the gap were, for the most part, standing on dry land. The Columbia was once again flowing freely from British Columbia to the Pacific Ocean. Almost fifty years of no maintenance and an equal time span of unusual seismic activity had erased some of the mightiest structures ever created by man.

That evening, just as the group had finished eating they were approached by an elderly man who asked to speak with Chris. The man introduced himself as Dr. Steven McDowell. He told Chris that he had just finished reading a biography written about Chris by Linda Ann. Steven mentioned the vapor trail seen by Chris in April of 2113 and said he had an explanation for that event. Steven had been a member of a team of engineers and scientists. They had rebuilt an aircraft for super long range flight, equipped with a remote control system and high resolution cameras, then launched it on a flight to look at the east coast of the U.S. They had flown it out over the Atlantic then began a wide right turn to bring it back to the coast. Their intention was to turn the plane north and fly up the coast as far as New England then turn it west towards California. While the plane was in the middle of its turn they experienced a major quake in their local area. The event destroyed much of their laboratory including their antennas. All contact with the plane was lost and they concluded that it had continued circling until it had run out of fuel and then crashed into the ocean. Chris thanked Steven for answering a question he had been carrying around for forty-two years. Steven was invited to sit with them. He told them he had a business proposition he would like to discuss if they had a few minutes to spare. He told them that when he had drifted north from California there was no work in his field of education and expertise. He had found and rehabilitated a twenty-five foot boat and become a fisherman. It turned out that he had a natural flair for catching salmon and soon was bringing in enough fish to trade for other necessities. With the fall of the dams and the subsequent access to their old spawning streams the salmon numbers rebounded to numbers not seen for two hundred years. Steven now had two sixty-five foot boats rigged for trawling and a number of smaller ones used for long line fishing. His crews seldom fished more than one day per week which was enough to provide all of the fish the local population could consume. His proposal was that if the people in Iowa could provide the aircraft he was prepared to ship a substantial amount of both fresh and frozen salmon. In another year it could include canned salmon as well. Craig and Billie said they could provide two planes immediately and Chris added that he thought in a matter of months they could have four aircraft dedicated to the northwest trade. He added that on returning home they would select some men to fly to Bellingham and meet with Steven and his group. They could settle on prices and what items were needed by the northwest people.

When the group gathered to board the plane the next morning there was an almost palpable feeling of energy among them. They were about to undertake a new endeavor and Chris voiced the opinion there would soon be highway and railroad crews working to reconstruct the land routes to the northwest. The plane lifted off at 7:00 am. The plan for the day was to fly over Grand Coulee again so everyone could see the devastation there then head directly to the Yellowstone area. From Yellowstone they would take a course to Rapid City and land at the Rapid City regional airport. Their meals for the next two days would be sandwiches and salads prepared in Bellingham. After a low flight over the ruins of Grand Coulee the mood in the plane became somber. The power of nature was almost too much to comprehend. The destruction of the dam and the California cities left them all with a sense of vulnerability and that the path of their future was, in a large part, out of their control. They arrived over the Yellowstone area and were again amazed. There was no indication of any thermal activity and no signs of any seismic events since Chris and Brendon had taken pictures of the area twenty-nine years ago. Instead of the huge basin seen in 2126 there was now a lake which they estimated to be at least sixty miles long by thirty miles wide. They made two circles around the lake then Billie turned the plane to the east and set a course for Rapid City.

They arrived in mid-afternoon and were surprised at the activity taking place. There were a half dozen planes parked in front of a hangar. Two of them, both prop planes, had their engines turning over while another was being taxied toward the runway. As they were getting off the plane they were met by a woman of perhaps 35 or 40 years who introduced herself as Lori Nolt she told them she was the airport manager which meant she got to empty the waste baskets once a week and sweep the floors at the same time. She told them they were the first non-local flight in the two years the airport had been open. There were a number of ranchers and farmers who had moved into the areas east and north of Rapid City. Those who lived more than fifty miles from town commuted primarily by small plane. Fuel was provided by a small refinery which had been reopened in Pierre. The rural people were becoming anxious about when the highways and railroads were going to be opened to their area. Lori then told the group if they would prefer to sleep in beds rather than on the office floor there was a motel just about a mile up the road. It had only been open for two weeks but it had a small dining room. She would need to call ahead if they decided to sleep and eat at the Black Hills Inn. Lori then told them she had two vans so she could transport all of them at the same time. She would leave one of the vans with them so they would not feel trapped at the Inn. As they were driving to the Inn, Lori asked if she could sit and eat supper with them. She had a story to tell and she thought Chris in particular would find it interesting.

When they drove into the parking area of the Inn the travelers were not impressed. There were a dozen cottages arranged around one side of a small circular lake of perhaps 2 acres in size. The lake was dry and the bed filled with dead cattails. The grass was burned brown and the cottages were all in dire need of painting. On entering the office they were greeted by a woman of about 60 years of age who told them her name was Kathleen and welcomed them as the first guests of the Black Hills Inn. She told them as the first customers of the Inn their visit would be on the house. The office as well as the cottages she showed them were all spotlessly clean and well furnished. Kathleen explained that she, her daughter and her grandson had spent 3 years refurbishing the interiors and when they could find a source for exterior paint they would start on the outside work. Kathleen, she told them to call her Kate, announced that supper would be ready at 6:30 and asked if they would prefer grilled pork chops or fried chicken. She warned them not to expect coffee or tea as they had been out of those American staples for three years. Billie immediately spoke up and said they had 20 pounds of coffee on the plane and at least 10 of tea. He told Kate he would drive to the airport and pick up some of both. Kate stepped over and clasped Billie in a long hug. She had tears in the corners of her eyes as she told him how welcome those two items would be. Billie told her to thank Uncle Chris as he had insisted he was not going on a 4 or 5 day trip without his morning coffee and afternoon tea. Lori drove Billie back to the airport to pick up the tea and coffee. When they returned it was apparent they were involved in a deep conversation. They went to seats in a corner and the conversation continued. They sat next to each other at the supper table and it became obvious to the group that something other than business was going on between the two. When they had finished eating and were chatting over coffee Billie addressed the three older couples and asked if it would be possible to stay over for a day or perhaps two. He had a business proposition to present and wanted to discuss it with them before they left Rapid City. The elders huddled and decided that none of them had anything waiting at home which couldn't be put on hold for two days. Calls were made via the satellite phone to let the people in Iowa know why they would be delayed for two days. At this point Carol told Lori that it was now time to hear her story.

Chapter 45 ----- 2155

As Lori stood to address the group, Chris, who was seated at the end of the table suggested she trade places with him so all of the group could hear her better. Carol, who was seated on the corner next to Chris asked Billie to trade seats with her. She patted him on the arm as they passed and told him she and Chris liked to sit where they could hold hands through any kind of a group meeting.

Lori opened her remarks by telling the group she had paperwork to verify everything she was going to tell them. She had letters, diaries, birth, death and marriage certificates plus pictures, many pictures. She told them much of the material or at least good copies should go to the Weddle family. Lori then told Chris if he went back six generations his grandfather from that generation, the first Elliott, had, in 1982, married her grandmother from that time whose name was Carol Ann Hamley. Carol Ann's daughter who was 20 at that time was the first Lori. The name had been carried on through the subsequent generations as Elliott had been with the Weddles. She added that she felt that made she and Chris step-cousins at least. She had gleaned from the diaries and letters that the first Lori had the first Elliott as a teacher at least once a year from the 7th through the 12th grade. After they were married Elliott and Carol Ann were discussing Lori's school years when he made the comment that she had been a "little shit" when she was in school. He then added that now she was his "little shit" and they understood each other so they got along fine. That sobriquet was attached to every Lori in the subsequent generations. Most of them wore it as a badge of honor although some of them were not aware of the origin of the epithet. Lori then told the group she knew most of their history and wanted them to know hers. She told them she had been born in Tuba City, Arizona in 2119. There was a community of about 25 people living in the area. They subsisted by growing large gardens and harvesting the wild cattle which were common in the area. Her parents, named Paul and Lori Russell, had met in Flagstaff as teenagers on the day after the world ended. They stayed in Flagstaff and lived off the bones of the city. After 3 years they declared themselves married and began living as man and wife. In 2112, after many discussions, the young couple decided they were going to travel north and east in search of other survivors. Their progress was slow. Lori insisted she was not leaving without the old steamer trunk which had been in her family for generations. It contained the history of her family and she was adamant about not leaving it behind. Paul found a small four wheeled cart with hard rubber tires and a brake system which was controlled by a rope and lever. On level ground one of them could pull the cart and they took turns. Going uphill required the efforts of both of them with frequent rest stops. They were exhausted when, after 12 days, they reached the intersection of the road leading to Tuba City. They decided to detour into the town and look for a house where they could rest under shelter for 2 or 3 days. It took them most of a day to reach the town. There they were elated to be met by a couple who said they were searching for their milk cow which had strayed during the day. The couple introduced themselves as Steve and Peggy White and said they had been living in Tuba City for 6 years. They told Paul and Lori there were 26 other people living in the city and that they all lived in the same neighborhood which was in the southwest side of town. When told of Paul and Lori's plan to find a house where they could rest for 2 or 3 days Peggy spoke up. She said there was a house next door to their own which had been cleaned and would need only a light dusting to be made livable. She added there was solar power plus a working well so they could rest in comfort. As they walked toward the area of the homes the wayward cow was spotted lying in a shady spot lazily chewing her cud. Steve called to her and told her to come along. The cow, named Gwen, got to her feet and followed them down the street. Steve commented that Gwen would most likely have returned home on her own at milking time. Steve had trapped her as a calf and she was more of a pet than a working milk producer. As the 2 couples approached home they met and talked to a number of people who welcomed the newcomers to the neighborhood. One of the, a woman who appeared to be 65 or 70, told them she hoped they would decide to stay permanently as the community needed more young people. Paul and Lori were shown to a 3 bedroom 2 bath house next door to the home of Steve and Peggy. The house was fully furnished and ready to be lived in. Peggy told them she had run the vacuum cleaner, mopped the bathrooms and kitchen plus thoroughly dusted less than a month before. She told them there was a supply of meat in the freezer and a variety of home canned fruits and vegetables in the pantry. They turned on the water heater and well pump then opened all of the water taps to purge the lines.

Supper that evening became a community affair with Steve and Peggy acting as hosts. A total of 14 people arrived bearing a variety of dishes to add to the meal. Paul and Lori were warmly welcomed. Almost without fail they were invited to become permanent residents. As they were preparing for bed that night Paul asked Lori what she thought of the idea of staying Tuba City permanently. Lori responded with the statement that she would love to remain in Tuba City. She had not realized how much she had missed the sound of other female voices. The couple announced their intention of staying and quickly became part of the little community. They soon had a garden planted. The other residents assured them that any produce which didn't have time to mature would be supplied to them by the already established gardeners. They planted enough to exceed their needs. Paul, who was an inveterate tinkerer soon found a nearly new electric/gasoline small truck. In a matter of days he had replaced the long dead battery and tuned up the gas engine. They were no longer tied to a traveling distance of a half day's walk from home. The years flowed by smoothly. Their primary concern was no medical doctor or medical facility of any kind. In January of 2119 Lori announced to Paul that she was pregnant and thought the baby would be born in September.

Chapter 46 ----- 2155

ori continued the story by reciting her own history. Two months before her birth on September 26, 2119 her father had been killed in an accident. An elderly woman had some sort of seizure and the electric car she was driving veered onto the sidewalk striking Paul and killing him instantly. The community rallied around the mother-to-be. She was provided food and household help. Several ladies attended her at the birth of her daughter. Peggy White was a skilled midwife and the birth occurred with no complications. On September 26, 2119 the newest Lori was welcomed to the world. In the tradition of her mother's family she was named Lori Ann Russell.

When Lori Ann was 3 months old Steve and Peggy saw the older Lori lying in her front lawn. They went to investigate and found her dead. On examining her body the found 2 puncture wounds in her arm which appeared to be fang marks from a snake bite. Not far from the body they found the severed head and body of a dead rattle snake. They surmised that the snake had been under a bush in the flower bed and had struck while Lori was pulling weeds. Because Lori's death had happened before she could get to the house they thought the fangs had punctured a vein, delivering the venom directly to the heart. Peggy entered the house to check on the baby and found her wet and hungry. She quickly changed the baby then looked for a bottle to prepare for Lori Ann. She remembered that the baby was being breast fed. She was breast feeding her own 5 month old son and felt she didn't have enough milk to feed both babies. Peggy solved that problem by deciding to alternate the little ones between breast feeding and a bottle of cow's milk. In the beginning both babies resisted the bottle but hunger soon brought that resistance to an end.

Lori now told the group that when she was 5, Steve and Peggy decided they must search until they found a community with a doctor and medical facilities. Steve had a van in which he had installed a twin battery system. While one battery was being used the other was being charged. It was a system of diminishing returns and eventually the van had to be plugged into a charging grid. The system worked well enough that the van could travel up to 1000 miles before needing to be connected to a charger.

They left Tuba City in early May. Traveling at a moderate speed they reached Kayenta. They spent the night in their tent in a roadside campground. The next day they reached the Four Corners area where Steve found a solar powered charging facility. They stayed at Four Corners for two days to let the 2 children rest and stretch their legs after 2 days of being cooped up in the van. They then spent 3 days in crossing the mountains to Walsenburg where again they spent 2 days resting. They had not seen another human in all that distance. Even at age 5 Lori would remember the grand visits of the Rockies and the torturous twisting roads leading up and down the passes. From Walsenburg they made the long drive to Lamar in one day. As they approached the town they began to see signs of people. There were irrigated fields of corn and wheat plus pastures holding cattle, horses and sheep. They stopped in front of what appeared to be a general store where, upon entering, they were greeted by a genial elderly couple. They soon were informed that the town held some 150 people including a doctor, 2 nurses and a dentist. They were told they would be welcomed to the community if they should choose to stay. The store owners were John and Mary Watson who had lived in the area even before the day of the red star. Steve and Peggy decided on the spot to stay in Lamar. Besides having a doctor and dentist there were children of the age of Lori and Patrick. Mary invited the travelers to spend the night in a cabin at the back of the store and said she would find someone to show them around the area where most of the Lamar residents lived. She assured them there were plenty of livable houses available needing only to be cleaned and dusted. When word was passed of the newcomers at the store at least two dozen people appeared to meet and welcome them. The next morning a steady stream of people appeared to add their welcome for the newcomers. They were assured when they decided on a house there would be more help than they needed to make it habitable. They settled on a 4 bedroom house. It would allow both children to have their own room and give Peggy a room for her sewing. Some beds and other furniture had to be replaced but with at least 15 people helping the house was pronounced ready to be lived in by mid-afternoon. While they were working on the house two small planes passed overhead. Steve who was both a veteran pilot and highly skilled mechanic asked about them. He was told there was a small local airport.

Two days after moving in Peggy was approached by a middle aged couple who asked her if she was interested in schooling for the two children. The couple, Carolyn and Jack Johansen, had been teachers before the "day" and for the past 10 years had been operating an informal school out of the house next door to their own. Peggy was elated with the prospect of school for the children. She pointed out that she had been working with them for over a year and both Lori and Patrick knew the alphabet and numbers. Both of them could read and write simple words and do addition of small numbers. With the children in school, which they both loved attending, Peggy let it be known that she was available to do custom sewing. Steve had made his way to the airport where, to his great surprise, he found an office, hangars and repair shop of what had been an aircraft dealership. In the hangar were two single engine 4 place planes plus a twin engine aircraft capable of carrying 10 passengers and baggage. All three of the planes were brand new but had been sitting for 20 plus years. Steve claimed the facility and set about cleaning it. Years of blown in dust had accumulated and there were 7 skeletons to be disposed of. It took him 2 months to finish the cleaning, then he began restoring the aircraft to flying condition. He replaced all of the fluids in the various systems and installed new hoses. Even the solid tires on the landing gear had developed flat spots. Steve solved this problem by mounting the wheels on a lathe and turning the tires round again. Initially he worked on only the single engine planes. With the planes up on wing jacks and using battery power, he cycled the landing gear to insure it would work. There was a 10 thousand gallon fuel storage tank which appeared to be full. Steve towed the planes outside, fueled them and started the engines for the first time in 20 years. Over a period of 3 days he started the engines and let them run at various speeds until the fuel ran dry. When he was satisfied that all of the systems were functioning as they should he began extensive taxi tests with the aircraft. Taking the planes to just below takeoff speed he checked all of the flight controls until he was convinced that they all worked properly. It was now the middle of the winter of 2124-2125.

Winters were becoming increasingly severe and Steve decided to delay his test flights until spring. He stayed busy all winter doing auto and truck repairs plus restoring the twin engine plane to flight condition. The winter passed rapidly and was a surprisingly mild one. Peggy was kept busy and was amazed at the number of customers who wanted her to sew for them. They paid primarily with canned and frozen garden produce plus a variety of baked goods. The two children were thriving in school. The teachers reported that their math and reading skills were already at a third grade level. At Peggy's urging Steve drove to every town within 100 miles looking for material from which Peggy could make clothing. He told her that when spring came he would try to find landing spots in Pueblo and Colorado Springs where there might be a bigger selection.

In April, like everyone else they planted a large garden. The gardens were located along the banks of the Arkansas River to insure an ample supply of water for irrigation. Steve tried to fly 4 or 5 hours every day. He alternated between the 3 planes until he was completely comfortable with all of them.

In May he was approached by two young men who asked him to teach them to fly. In exchange they offered to take care of the family garden and do all of the grunt work around the flight facility. The young men, their names were Rick and Jerry, had been born in 2106 and 2107. When the older of the two, Rick, was 14 their parents had been killed in a snow slide in the mountains western Colorado. They had been drifting since that time and wanted a place where they could settle and live a normal life.

Chapter 47 ----- 2155

ori continued her story. The years seem to flash past and by 2136 both Patrick and Lori were accomplished pilots. Lori had been digging into the information in her family trunk. She knew the family name from 7 generations past had been Nolt and that they had migrated from South Dakota to Oregon. She began using Nolt as her family name and expressed the wish to someday travel to South Dakota to see where her family had come from. In the spring of 2140 Steve told the family that if Lori really wanted to go to South Dakota he would fly her to Rapid City. If they found any people there she could stay but from that point she would be on her own. Peggy's eyesight was failing and he would not move her to an area of unknown medical facilities. There were many tears but Lori felt compelled to make the move. The flight was uneventful and they arrived to find the airport being used by several local pilots plus a number of farmers and ranchers from outlying areas. Steve stayed in Rapid City with Lori for 10 days. They found a small 2 bedroom house within walking distance of the airport, cleaned it up and got her moved in. At the airport terminal they found a small parking garage with a solar powered charging system. There were several vehicles plugged into the grid but on checking they found all of the batteries were long dead. Steve replaced the batteries in 2 vehicles and in 24 hours they were charged and ready for use. Lori told Steve she wanted to open an air service similar to what he had operating in Colorado. She would need to find a skilled aircraft mechanic and would put out the word to the locals immediately. Steve told her he thought Jerry was itching for a change of scenery and just might welcome the opportunity to move to Rapid

City. Sure enough, two months later a twin engine plane landed and taxied up to the front of the terminal building. Lori walked out to greet the new arrival. When the passenger door opened, out stepped Jerry who greeted her with, "I hear you are looking for a mechanic and I want to apply for the job." Jerry tried to shake hands but Lori grasped him in a fierce hug. She held him for a long time then stepped back and with tears in her eyes, told him how happy she was to see him. They proceeded to set Jerry up in a hangar which had a repair area equipped with a full set of tools and machines for aircraft maintenance and repair. He was soon busy with work from the local aircraft owners and the pilots from all of western South Dakota. When they heard that a small refinery had been restarted in Pierre Jerry rehabilitated a tanker truck and began hauling fuel to Rapid City. Neither Jerry nor Lori had much spare time so they hired a local man named Robert Myers to drive the tanker and help out in the maintenance area. The only cash money available was the new U.S. currency which had trickled in from back east. It was readily accepted everywhere but most debts were settled by bartering goods and services. In addition Lori had a box holding some 10 pounds of gold dust and nuggets which she had panned and sluiced from the Arkansas River as a child and teenager. Jerry also had a stash of gold although it was a smaller amount than Lori's.

The business slowly but steadily increased. They began making charter flights. Most of these were for business men with more than a few being for medical mercy flights. Lori concluded her remarks by saying that it had been 173 years since the marriage of their ancestors but she felt that she was now with family.

Chapter 48 ----- 2155

When Lori stopped speaking she took her seat. It was not lost on the group that Billie immediately took her hand in his and continued to hold it as Chris began to speak. Chris told Lori that she was indeed with family and that she was a welcome addition. The group sat around the table talking for an hour. Carol finally suggested that they needed to leave so Kate could close up and go home. Kate overheard this remark and told the group they could stay as long as they wished to talk. Having such a happy group as her first customers was a good omen and she didn't want to see it end.

At about 11:00 pm the group began to leave to go to their cabins. Kate told them to sleep in next morning and she would be ready to serve them breakfast at nine. Billie drove Lori to her home. He didn't arrive at the cabin he was sharing with Craig until 4:30 am. With less than four hours of sleep he arrived at breakfast and immediately told the group that he had an announcement which he would relate to them when Lori arrived. Carol nudged Chris and whispered, "Like father like son." Sure enough, when Lori arrived Billie stood and told the group that he and Lori were going to be married as soon as they could find someone to do the ceremony. He added, "Today if possible." Kate interjected that as soon as breakfast was finished, she, as an ordained minister of her church, would perform the wedding there in the restaurant. The wedding was over before noon with all of the papers signed and even notarized by Brendon who served in that capacity in Iowa. Billie announced that Lori would return to Iowa with them, then if his and Craig's business proposition was approved he and Lori would return to Rapid City to live.

Chris suggested that since they seemed to have taken over Kate's dining room they might as well have the meeting there immediately. The women all decided to go sightseeing while the men were discussing business. They boarded one of the vans and with Lori as their guide drove off to visit Mount Rushmore memorial.

Craig and Billie's presentation was short and to the point. They both felt there was going to be an increase in the movement of people and goods between the eastern population centers and the northwest. Until the highways and railroads were rebuilt the only way to accomplish that would be on foot or by air. They proposed starting a combined passenger and air freight service between Perry and Bellingham with a midway station at Rapid City. Billie would become the manager in Rapid City, Craig would do the same in Bellingham. They thought Jib's son Robert would welcome the job in Perry. He was young but the elders would be close at hand to lend support and advice. At present the group had 3 small twin engine planes capable of the flight from Perry to Bellingham non-stop. There were now 3 engine medium sized planes being produced in Wichita which were being sold at a low price due to low demand. Chris asked the two younger men to step outside while the 3 older ones discussed the idea. When they were outside Billie turned to Craig and told him the older men were not going to buy into their scheme. It was going to require too much of a cash outlay to get started. Craig laughed and said, "You don't know my dad. He is bored and so is Uncle Brendon. We are on this trip because Mom and Aunt Phoebe asked me to get Dad and Uncle Brendon out of the house and interested in something new. There is enough family money to finance this operation many times over. They will both want to be involved but they will allow us to make the major decisions." After an hour Craig and Billie were asked to return inside. Chris acted as the spokesman for the elders. He said they had decided the plan had merit but it would require extensive studies before it could be implemented.

During supper that evening Kate surprised the bride and groom with a 3 tiered wedding cake complete with the miniature bride and groom on top. After the cake was cut and toasts were made to the new couple Chris asked Kate to come out of the kitchen as he had an announcement which concerned her. When she was seated with the group Chris told her that as a token of appreciation for her generosity and hospitality he wanted to send a crew to refurbish the grounds and the outsides of the cabins. All he needed to know was the color of paint for the cabins. He added that the crew would clean the dead rushes from the bottom of the little lake and rig a system to pump water from the nearby stream to fill the lake. There was already a natural outlet and the constant circulation would keep the water fresh. By this time Kate was in tears. She arose from her seat, clasped Chris in a long hug and kissed him soundly on the cheek. She then echoed the words used many times by Carol when she said, "You are a good man Mr. Weddle." After this exchange they all began to return to their respective cabins. It was a warm balmy evening and by unplanned agreement they carried deck chairs from the front porches of the cabins and arranged them around a circular fir pit in front of the cabins. There was no need for a fire but the arrangement was ideal for conversation. There was some discussion of the future and what their world might look like in fifty years.

The youngsters, Dallon and Phoebe, wanted to hear about life prior to the day the old world ended. They also asked questions of Chris and Carol about their monumental walks in the west and in Mexico. Chris then commented that in the 40 plus years he had known her he had never heard Melinda's story of her years in the dead city of Chicago or her walk from there to her people in South Dakota. He added that it was a part of their collective history and should be recorded for the enlightenment of future generations. Melinda replied that it was a dark time of her life on which she didn't like to dwell. She did promise that after they arrived home she would go to her computer and write the story of those 3 years when she was alone. Brendon and Phoebe spoke of finding each other in eastern Oregon and almost instantly deciding to go to the Skagit Valley in Washington. Brendon was a young farmer with a degree in Agricultural Science from Washington State University and he said Phoebe had more common sense than two people should be entitled to possess. Chris exacted a promise from both Brendon and Phoebe to record their memoirs after they reached New Home.

Billie collected his bag from the cabin he had been sharing with Craig then he and Lori departed for her home. It was a very small house and they agreed that when they returned from New Home they would search for a larger residence.

The next morning the group began inspecting the buildings at the airport with the hope of finding one which would meet their needs. They wanted a facility which would provide maintenance and storage areas as well as a small passenger terminal. Lori suggested that her offices were large enough to serve as a passenger terminal and also office space for Billie and whatever staff he might require. After inspecting the entire facility Lori was offered a partnership in the yet unnamed company. Jerry was offered the job of chief mechanic. He laughed and said it would be the first job in his life for which he would be paid and actual salary. With their office and maintenance space needs settled they began looking for a building which would serve as a storage facility. Just adjacent to the airport they found a 20,000 square foot warehouse. Half of the building was filled with shelving still holding a variety of merchandise. The other half of the building had been a cold storage facility. Brendon who had some experience with similar facilities thought this one could be cleaned up and restarted. With their facility search ended the group returned to Kate's restaurant and began compiling manpower lists to accomplish not only their own needs but to refurbish Kate's cabins and the lake. It soon became apparent that it was going to require many flights of the three planes they had available. They decided to immediately purchase 2 of the 3 engine planes being built at the plant in Wichita. Jerry was asked and agreed to live in Lori's home until she and Billie returned from Iowa. This was to insure that no one would move into the home or enter and go through her possessions.

The flight to Iowa the next day was uneventful. They arrived in Perry in early afternoon and were met by Kathie, Letha and Aaron. These 3 announced that Wolf Song dinner was to be held that night. It was to be held at the picnic shelter. Chris Jr. and Mavis were at the shelter preparing ribs and a ham from Brendon Jr's. smokehouse. Mavis had used Phoebe's recipe to make potato salad and Linda Ann had prepared chocolate pies form Carol's recipe. There would be fresh vegetables from the gardens.

Chapter 49 ----- 2155

Attendance at the Wolf Song supper that evening was the largest in the history of the event. The clan had gathered from all over the Midwest. There were 58 men, women and children present. Linda Ann had driven to Carroll to pick up Doreen Wilhelm. At age 83 Doreen was the oldest of the group and as such she was given the seat of honor at the head of the main table. Chris, Brendon and Brad had, over the years, been taking turns as master of ceremonies. Tonight was Brendon's turn. He took the microphone for the little PA system which had been set up and welcomed every one. He thanked Mavis who had, at age 9, named the gathering and by extension the community as well. Brendon then introduced Lori to the group and asked she and Billie to stand. Brendon asked the pair if they wanted to speak to the group and on receiving affirmative nods passed the mike to them. Lori took the microphone and thanked the group for the warm welcome she had been given. As she started to pass the mike to Billie she stopped and spoke again. She said, "Just so everyone knows, I am positive I am pregnant." There was applause and some hooting from the younger people. Billie took the mike and with a wide smile told the gathering that he had heard the family stories and he was only trying to live up to the standards which had been set by his father and Uncle Chris.

After they had eaten and cleared the tables Lori told those sitting near her about her treasured trunk holding the documents and pictures. She told them when she and Billie were settled she would have copies made and they could see the connections between her family and the Weddles 170 years in the past. As people began asking Lori about her personal history Brendon asked for their attention. He then told the group that Lori had told them her life history in Rapid City. He said they had her life story on a disc and with her permission they would make it available to anyone who wanted to hear it. Brendon then apologized to Lori for taping her story without first asking for her approval. Lori was surprised at the announcement but nodded her assent. It would be a better arrangement than answering the same questions over and over. They sat and visited until it was almost full dark. As if on cue the wolf song began. Surprisingly it sounded as it had in years past, with several of the big predators joining in the chorus. When the song ended the people started gathering their belongings and departing for home or wherever they were spending the night. It was love at first sight with Lori and the house built by Billie's parents. She made the comment that she wished they had this house in Rapid City. Billie replied that they could stay in Iowa. He felt confident that Jerry was fully capable of managing the facility in Rapid City. They had been invited to have breakfast with the elder Weddles and Hintzs in the morning. When they were walking to the Weddle house Lori asked Billie if they really could live in Iowa. She had been so impressed with the people she had met the night before that she wanted to get to know them better. Billie was surprised by her remarks but told her if that was what she wanted he would do his best to make it happen.

When Billie told Chris and Brendon what they had discussed he was told that the elders had been having the same discussion. It was decided over breakfast. Billie would stay in Perry, Craig would go to Bellingham and they would find someone with business experience to assist Jerry in Rapid City.

The schedules of everyone involved in the airline venture became hectic. Brad and Melinda both had backlogs of patients to see after being away for ten days. Chris hired a crew of 15 men for the rehab of the cabins and lake in Rapid City. He also bought paint, coffee and basic kitchen supplies for Kate. It would require two trips for each of their three available planes to transport the men, their tools and the materials needed to do the work. He was also sending 25 of the satellite phones and a radio to insure constant and instant communication between Rapid City and Perry. The same equipment would be sent to Bellingham when the planes were available for Craig to make the move to that city. Five of the men hired to work on the motel were hired because of their experience with cold storage facilities. When work on the motel was completed they would move to the warehouse and cold storage building to investigate whether it could be started again.

Brendon chartered a local plane and flew to Wichita to look at the planes being built here. He was impressed with the speed, cargo capacity, and the short runway capabilities of the aircraft. When he returned home Brendon met with Chris and they decided to purchase three of the planes. Two of them would be combination passenger, cargo craft while the third would be strictly a cargo carrier. During a meeting of Brendon, Brad and Chris they were interrupted by their wives. Melinda told the men there was a problem which demanded immediate attention. Phoebe then took over. She reminded the men of the excursion the women had taken when the group was in Rapid City. They had gone to visit Mt. Rushmore and Crazy Horse monuments, both of which had suffered serious degradation after 50 years of no maintenance. The women had already spoken with George and Martha of the Hintz Construction Company. Both of them had agreed to attempt to restore both monuments at cost if the government would pay for the labor and materials. George, who was very imaginative and creative had some ideas of how the restoration could be accomplished. Chris and Brendon who knew many people in the government agreed to approach the Secretary of the Interior with the proposal and ask if the government would finance the operation.

Chapter 50

2155

Six experienced pilots were hired and sent to Wichita to be checked out in the new planes. The planes would not be delivered until October and November but they wanted the pilots trained and ready before the planes were on hand. Also hired were six pilots for the three planes now flying. Craig and Billie were going to have other duties which would not leave them time for frequent flights.

The rest of the summer seemed to pass in a blur. The crew hired to complete the work at the Black Hills motel made rapid progress. By the middle of September they had finished work on the cabins. The little lake bed had been cleaned out and the pumps installed to fill it with water. With work at the motel completed most of the crew went to work rehabbing nearby houses. The work required was much more extensive than had been needed 35 and 40 years ago in Iowa and other eastern areas. There were many homes which would have to be demolished. As a side note to the rehab effort, James Peterson who had been named foreman of the repair crew and who at age 60 was a master carpenter immediately fell head over heels for Kate. It soon became apparent that the feeling was mutual and they made plans to be married as soon as the job was completed.

Craig, Chris, Carol and a half dozen workmen flew to Bellingham to check on available facilities and housing possibilities. They checked with the fishermen who were supplying the population with a full variety of seafood. The fishermen and crabbers assured them that the supply of seafood was more than adequate to feed the entire U.S. population. After 50 years of no appreciable harvest the various fish and crab populations had rebounded to numbers not seen in 250 years. There was a cannery and freezer plant lacking only customers to increase production. Chris and Craig settled on the hangar and shop which had been used prior to the move east in 2116 and 2117. Chris made a note to himself to ask Jinx and his son to revive the auto landing systems plus the landing and taxi lights at both Bellingham and Rapid City.

They had brought a short wave radio which was set up in the hangar office. They also left 25 satellite phones to be distributed to the local population with the promise of more once they began flight operations. The 2 doctors operating a small clinic gave them a list of medicines and medical supplies which were badly needed. Perhaps the most welcome item the group brought to Bellingham was 20 pounds of coffee. They left half of it at the little restaurant near the airport and distributed the rest among the local residents. They accepted orders for coffee, clothing and various household items with the promise they would be delivered within the next month.

Chapter 51 -----2155

Rapid City was bypassed on the way home so they arrived in Perry in the middle of the afternoon.

With the organization of the little airline underway and Hintz Construction studying the restoration of the monuments in the Black Hills, the elders met and came to a major decision. They were all past 70 years of age and felt it was time to retire. This meant turning the decision making over to the next generation. They decided to name a 5 member board to oversee the various group endeavors. A chairman was to be appointed by a vote of the board members and would serve in that capacity for 10 years. Retirement would be mandatory at age 70 with a replacement being named for the board.

The 5 member board consisted of Chris Jr., Craig, Brendon Jr., Aaron and Billie. Chris Jr. was elected to be the first chairman. Linda Ann, who now had a growing law practice, was recruited to become the corporate attorney for the group. The name New Home Enterprises was selected for the new entity. To honor Chris a logo was designed which depicted a man and 3 dogs walking down a highway.

In October an engineering firm was hired to design a refrigeration unit which was both small and light enough to be installed in one of the twin engine planes. The purpose was to enable the transport of fresh fish and seafood from the northwest.

Also in October Billie and Lori flew to Colorado to visit Lori's adoptive parents, Steve and Peggy. Lori referred to them as Mom and Dad as they were the only parents she had ever known.

Upon their arrival in Lamar they were surprised to find the older couple living in almost total seclusion. Peggy's eyesight had deteriorated to the point where she was functionally blind. Steve stayed at home to care for her. He had arranged furniture and put up handrails to enable her to move from room to room. She required help selecting clothing, getting dressed and even eating became a major trial. There were no doctors or health facilities in the area capable of diagnosing or treating the problem. Peggy and Steve told Lori they had not informed her of the problem because she had gone through enough trauma in her life and they wanted her to enjoy her future with her new husband. Lori immediately took charge. She told them she and Billie lived fifty miles from one of the best medical centers in the U.S. She wanted to take them to Ames and have Peggy examined by experts. She promised them that when Peggy was finished with the doctors the older couple would be flown back to Lamar or if they chose they would be welcome to stay in New Home. Lori reminded them there was going to be a grandchild in late March or early April and they might want to be present for that event. That statement removed any lingering reluctance and Steve told Lori she could help her mother pack. They remained in Lamar for a week. Because of the uncertainty of the length of their stay in Iowa Steve was diligent in gathering all of Peggy's must keep possessions. Patrick, who was married and lived nearby, took a number of items to store in his home. He also promised to check once a week in an effort to insure the house remained in good shape.

Upon arriving home Lori soon had Peggy set up for appointments with the appropriate doctors. A month of exams and test was followed by a statement from the doctors. Peggy was told that a corneal transplant should restore her eyesight. She might require eyeglasses but her sight would be restored to an acceptable level. In December a donor became available and the surgery was performed. Peggy was ecstatic with the results. She did not require corrective lenses and claimed she could see better than at any time in her life. Peggy related to Lori that in their years together she had taught Lori many things. She then added that those things did not include caring for a baby or child rearing. In light of that Peggy felt she and Steve needed to stay in New Home to assist with the baby. Chris told the couple they were welcome to move into the house he had provided for Lisa Myers during her years in New Home. It had been empty since her passing. Chris told them he would deed the house to them if they wanted the permanence of the deed. Two of the planes were sent to Lamar to bring the remaining possessions which Peggy felt she needed to make her home truly her own.

Chapter 52 ----- 2156

The beginning of the new year was reminiscent of the early 20's. On January 2 it turned bitterly cold and it began to snow. The snow was accompanied by strong winds. The snow and winds continued unabated for 5 days. When the storm finally ended there was over 2 ½ feet of snow on the ground. Almost every road in Iowa and surrounding states was closed. In places the drifts were twelve to fifteen feet high and had been hard packed by the wind. Even the railroads had been brought to a standstill. Almost every cut in the terrain which had been made to level the road bed was full of hard packed snow. With the machines available it would take weeks to clear the roads and rail lines. A number of people perished in the storm including two families with small children who became trapped on the highway. As the weather cleared search groups went out. Using snow machines they went to remote or isolated homes and found more victims of the storm. A few more bodies were discovered. Several of these victims were elderly people who had ventured outside for some purpose and for whatever reason had been unable to return to the safety of their homes. The situation was repeated all over the mid-west. From the lake states south into Kentucky and from eastern Nebraska to western Pennsylvania the land was locked in an icy grip. The final death count was settled at 188 but it was suspected there were still uncounted bodies which would add to the total. The event became known as "The Great Storm of 56" and would be vividly remembered by everyone who lived through it.

Chapter 53 ----- 2156

By the middle of February life had just about returned to normal in New Home. After the January storm the winter had become surprisingly mild with only a couple of light snows and moderate temperatures.

The flights between Perry and Bellingham had become immediately successful. There was a small but steady stream of people moving from Iowa to the northwest. Most of this population was made up of people and their children who had moved to Iowa during the exodus of 2116. The soil in Washington was no more productive than what they had in Iowa but they fondly remembered the mild winters and cooler summers. There was also a significant number who wanted to resume a life of fishing and harvesting the bounty of other seafoods from Puget Sound and northern waters.

George and Martha had taken a crew to Rapid City. They had erected temporary construction villages at both monuments and were studying the most practical approach to repair both sites. They had developed a composite cement which hardened to the density of concrete while having less than 1/10 the weight. This material was also being considered for use in repairing roads and bridges.

The federal government, which was paying for the project, had determined to use old Interstate 90 as the route to the northwest. They began assembling men, tools and equipment in Sioux Falls in preparation for the spring weather which would allow them to start west across the plains. The rail route had a lower priority than the highway. It was estimated the rail project would require 7 to 8 years to complete.

Chapter 54 ----- 2156

By the first of March Lori's pregnancy was a common topic of conversation in the Wolf Song community. Her abdomen had become huge. Carol and Melinda convinced Lori to come to the clinic and submit to an ultrasound. The test revealed that Lori was carrying twins, a girl and a boy and that both were developing normally. On the same day Mavis and Jonathon's daughter-in-law Carolyn, who was married to their son Christopher, also underwent an ultrasound. Carolyn's test showed that she was carrying a little boy. The test also showed that this baby was a Down's Syndrome child. Carolyn was riding with Billie and Lori and she wept all the way to New Home where she and Chris lived. Lori attempted to comfort Carolyn all of the way home, to no avail. As Carolyn was getting out the of car she turned and said, "Don't misunderstand, I am not crying because the baby has Down's Syndrome but because I know what a struggle life will be for him. I only wish I could carry some of the burden for him." After Billie escorted Carolyn into her house he returned to the car to find Lori in tears also. When Billie asked her what was wrong she replied, "Absolutely nothing. It doesn't matter how severe that little boy's affliction turns out to be, he is going to be showered with enough love and attention to overcome the obstacles. I predict he will become a productive and respected member of our community."

In the middle of March, Chris went out one morning to stoke the fire in the smokehouse. He had a hundred pounds of salmon in the process of smoking and was anxious to see how it would turn out. When he returned to the house he felt faint, he had broken into a cold sweat and was feeling pressure in his chest.

Carol, who happened to be home that morning, made him sit down then gave him 2 nitro tablets from her ever present medical case and put an oxygen mask on him. She then called for an ambulance and sat holding his hand until it arrived. Carol called the Cardiologist who had an office in her clinic and asked him to meet them at the hospital. To say Chris received special treatment was probably true. Carol insisted on it and she carried a lot of weight in the medical community. After 3 days of diagnostic tests Chris was informed that he had substantial blockage in arteries in his chest and his groin area. In the end the Cardiologist placed 4 stents in his chest and 2 in each femoral artery. Carol assured the Cardiologist that Chris would adhere to the diet plans and that he would be doing a lot more walking.

By the first of April it was apparent that the delivery dates for both Lori and Carolyn were very near.

Chapter 55 ----- 2156

April 7 had been designated as a National Holiday. There were no parades, fireworks or speeches. Instead it had become a day for meditation of the past and of the event which had changed all of their lives.

The Wolf Song community had, for the past few years, used the day to gather and discuss their lives and families. They included the families of those people who had survived the early days with them. The meetings often exceeded 70 people. The picnic shelter where they gathered had twice been expanded so they could be under a roof when the weather was bad.

They were almost ready to eat when Lori stiffened in her chair, groaned, then said, "I think you will have to eat without us." Billie soon had her in his car and they were on their way to the hospital, followed closely by Steve and Peggy. At the hospital they found Carolyn already checked in and Christopher pacing in the waiting room. Billie insisted that he was going to sit in the room with Lori. When Christopher discovered that this was allowed he was soon in the room with Carolyn.

Brendon, Phoebe, Carol and Chris soon joined the group in the waiting room. Brendon and Phoebe were there to see a great-grandson join the family. Carol came because she felt responsible for the health of the entire extended family. Chris felt a need to be there as a surrogate for Billie's deceased parents, Pete and Jackie Brown.

The two women went in to labor at approximately the same time. At 4:47pm Lori delivered a 6 ½ pound girl followed 5 minutes later by a boy of the same weight. An hour later Carolyn delivered a 6 pound boy who, as predicted, was a Down's

Syndrome baby. The names for all three babies came directly out of the papers from Lori's treasured trunk. The twins were named Kathleen Verneice and Daniel Arthur. Carolyn knew of the past also so she and Billie named their son Cody Lee. Peggy, Carol and Phoebe each picked up a baby and all three were reluctant to surrender the infants to the nurses when it was feeding time.

Jonathon and Mavis who had been in South Dakota on tribal business arrived at 8:30 that evening. Christopher wanted his two brothers to share this glorious moment but they were both in South Dakota and could not be spared from their tribal tasks.

Finally, all of the group except the two new fathers were shooed out of the hospital and told not to return before nine the next morning. Phoebe and Mavis insisted they would sleep in chairs in the waiting room. Carol and the nurses told them that wherever they slept they would not be allowed to see either of the mother or the babies before nine in the morning so they might as well go home.

Chapter 56 ----- 2156

With the coming of spring the pace of life picked up all across the U.S. Farmers were working long hours to get crops planted. The building industry was booming as people began replacing the homes built before the "day." New manufacturing plants were being opened to produce consumer goods long missing from the market.

Progress on the highway project was rapid. The roadbed was in remarkably good shape after fifty years of no maintenance. Across South Dakota a total of five bridges had to be replaced. The largest of these was the span across the Missouri River at Chamberlin. The Hintz Construction Company was awarded the contract for the bridges and began work immediately. Work on the Black Hills monuments would have to wait for the opening of the highway. There was no other way to move the heavy materials required for the job.

Kenneth Thompson had been one of Jonathon's companions when the five young men had brought the news that the Cheyenne people were moving from the Rio Grande to Iowa was now the elected Chief of the tribe. On his election had had taken the name Running Man as was the custom of the Cheyenne. He was now sixty years old and gray haired but he was still vigorous and full of life.

One day Running Man appeared at the door of Chris and Carol where he explained the he needed some advice. Over lunch on the deck Running Man explained his mission. He told them he knew Chris had been the moving force who had settled the Cheyenne on the rich farm land in Iowa and insured their acceptance into the society. With a sigh he added that his people were people of the plains. Even after forty plus years the Cheyenne still longed to return to the prairie. Life would be harder for them but it was what the majority wanted. For the past 5 years there had been scouts exploring what had been Cheyenne territory 300 years in the past. They had settled on a strip on land in eastern Colorado. It would be bordered by Kansas and Nebraska on the east and north. By highway 50 on the south and highway 71 on the west. The land was essentially empty, being occupied by herds of wild cattle, horses and a substantial population of bison. They would rehabilitate the little town of Yuma, build a hospital, schools and an airport. Running Man said he did not want to appear ungrateful but this was what his people wanted and he felt obliged to try and make it come about.

Chris suggested that the place to start looking for approval of the major undertaking would be with the Secretary of the Interior. All unclaimed lands fell under the jurisdiction of the Interior Department. It would be crucial to have the support of Interior if such a large area was to be deeded to such a small number of people. Chris said the current Secretary was an old friend. She was a dedicated worker who had been a young intern in the days when the Cheyenne, the California people and later the immigrants from South Africa and Israel were being settled. She had made the job her life's work and 3 years ago had been confirmed as the Secretary of the Interior Department. Chris told Running Man he would be happy to introduce him to the Secretary whose name was Jackie Schmidt. Chris said he would sit in on the meeting if Running Man wished him to do so. Otherwise the role Chris played would end with the introduction. Running Man was elated with the proposal and said he would be pleased to have Chris take part in the meeting and perhaps offer advice when needed.

Chris called Jackie, briefly explained and she cleared her calendar for two days in the following week.

The meeting went well. Jackie's two top aides sat in. They asked many questions and took many notes. Jackie asked Chris for his opinion on the move. Chris replied that while he didn't like the idea of losing so many good citizens he could understand the yearning of the Cheyenne people for their homeland. Chris recalled that in all of those terrible years when he was alone he never considered leaving his home in Iowa. Jackie thanked the two visitors for coming and promised Running Man she would have a response to his proposal within two weeks. She reminded him it would take an act of Congress to deed the proposed area to the Cheyenne.

True to her word, in less than the promised two weeks, Jackie called Running Man and asked for a meeting. She suggested they meet in his office in Carroll. She explained that she expected they were going to have a great deal of interaction and she wanted to meet his staff. Jackie quickly explained that despite her reservations to seeing the Cheyenne people leave Iowa she was going to support their request. She added that she had spoken with several influential legislators and it appeared as if the required legislation could be passed. Jackie did suggest one change to the boundaries of the proposal land grant. She pointed out that a substantial number of farmers and ranchers had settled in a strip twenty miles north and south of the Arkansas River. She proposed moving the southern border of the Cheyenne enclave some 45 miles north. The southern boundary of the Cheyenne land would be marked by US Highway 40 from the Nebraska state line to Arroyo and from there to Punkin Center by Colorado Route 94. If the Cheyenne would agree to this change Jackie was sure the legislation would proceed with little opposition. Running Man agreed to the change and assured her the tribe would not object.

Chapter 57 ----- 2156

It was early May on a balmy afternoon. Chris and Carol were sitting on the deck enjoying the sunshine and a glass of iced tea. They had both fallen into an introspective mood and had been discussing the bad old days following the "Day" when their world had ended. They also discussed the possibilities for the future of their children and grandchildren. Chris commented that he regretted not having been able to do more for the future generations. Carol replied that he had been a major force in the building of the new United States and in particular the creation of the city of New Home where most of their extended family was living. Their discussion was interrupted when Brendon and Phoebe drove in unannounced. Brad and Melinda followed only minutes later. Brendon opened the conversation. He told them he had meant to speak at the gathering on April 7. The onset of Lori's labor pains and the resulting turmoil had negated his plans. Brendon said he wanted to thank Chris for bringing them all to Iowa. Brendon went on to say that second only to finding Phoebe in Oregon it was the best thing to happen in his life. The big man choked up and with tears in his eyes, took a seat. He was followed by Melinda who was weeping even before she started to speak. She hugged Chris fiercely and kissed him soundly. Through her tears she thanked him for taking her on the long walk to Washington where she had found Brad after not knowing if he was dead or alive.

Carol prepared sandwiches and a salad and the six old friends sat on the deck and talked of families, the past and conjectured on what the future might hold. The night birds began to chatter and with the onset of full dark they were treated to a chorus of wolf song. The three couples were reluctant to go their separate ways that night. It was unspoken but all of them were aware that, given their ages, there couldn't be many more years for these meetings.

As the visitors were leaving Brendon and Melinda each passed an envelope to Chris. They told him the envelope contained the recordings Chris had asked them to make of their experiences in the time following the day the world had ended in 2106.

It was late and Chris was tired. He decided that listening to the recordings would have to wait for a day when he was fresh and well rested. His eventual goal was to find someone to take these two stories plus his own journals and Carol's story and combine them into book form. He felt it was important that the younger generations learn what the elders had undergone to survive the dark days.

The author at his writing table, watching the Mariners

lliott Combs is a pseudonym for Harold Elliott Weddle. I grew up using Elliott as my name because of a preference by my mother. Her maiden name was Combs. When a friend insisted that I must have a pen name, my grandfather William Daniel Combs came to mind. The military insisted on first names, so everyone I have met since 1952 knows me as Harold.

I grew up in the little Iowa town of Dawson. After a hitch in the Air Force, I enrolled and graduated from Clemson University in South Carolina. I spent the next 31 years teaching various Industrial Arts classes plus Math and U.S. History.

When I started writing in 2012, I decided to make Dawson and later Mount Vernon prominent locales in the book. Many of the names used are those of family and friends, but not necessarily in the content of when I knew them in the past.

There is no scientific proof of anything written here, therefore, I don't expect to need to defend the story from "experts".

We live in a senior mobile home park. My typist who also lives here in the park has been wonderful. I worry about asking too much of her, but she continues to ask for more of the manuscript to type. Her name is Linda Keltz and I will never be able to thank her enough.

Elliott Combs

Mount Vernon, Washington

June 2014

32316166R00142

Made in the USA
Charleston, SC
11 August 2014